THE UNBORN

THE UNBORN
A FANTASY NOVEL

by

KENNETH C. STEVEN

JANUS PUBLISHING COMPANY
London, England

First published in Great Britain 1992 by
Janus Publishing Company

© Kenneth C. Steven 1991

British Library Cataloguing in Publication Data

Steven, Kenneth C., *1968–*
   The unborn.
   I. Title
   823.914 [F]
   ISBN 1 85756 040 X

All rights reserved
Unauthorised duplication
contravenes existing laws.

Cover design David Murphy

Phototypeset by Intype, London
Printed in Great Britain by
Antony Rowe Ltd,
Chippenham, Wiltshire

For my Mother and Father – for their never-ending faith

Contents

Part I Rebirth   1
        1. The First Winter   3
        2. Childhood   10
        3. The Caves of Half-life   16
        4. Peter   24
        5. The Rock of Sacrifice   32
        6. The Snows   41
        7. Celroc   51
        8. Mount Gilrene   60

Part II The Healing of Spring   67
        1. The King   69
        2. Return   78
        3. The Shadow   84
        4. The Reed Lands   91
        5. Pyrus   99
        6. The Eternal Flame   106
        7. The Well   115
        8. Descent   120
        9. The Voice   127
            Epilogue   133

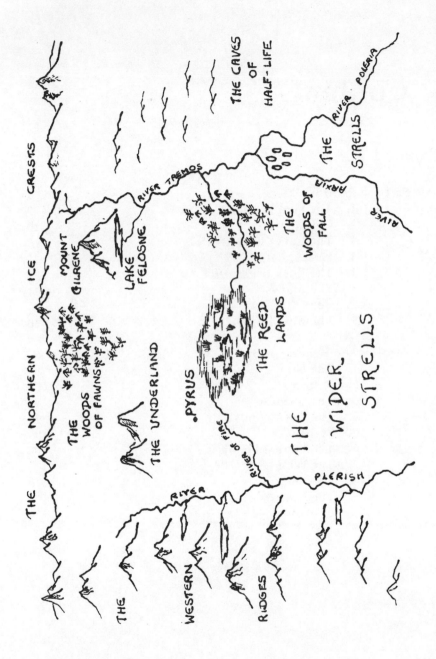

Part 1

Rebirth

Chapter 1

The First Winter

As the glory of the day had faded, the moon had risen to shine eerily over the quiet waters of the Eastern Sea. Its light had increased as the night hours passed, the long silver avenue reaching over to the island and the line of hills beyond. The only sounds were those of the ripples that fell and fell again on the island shore until even they seemed to be swallowed up in silence.

On the Well, the Well of Half-life, the moon shone doubly bright. Yet still its brilliance appeared to intensify, spilling over the water in ripple after ripple. Then, beneath the surface, there came a shadow, a shadow that seemed to struggle upwards towards the light; first, a pale hand grasping the air in a search for life; then, swiftly, the head of a child. For a moment his eyes were closed, as his first gasps broke the silence and the water streamed in rivulets from his body; his face was like a silver mask as he stood now in the moonlight, blinking in its brightness.

Then the waters of the Well drained strangely away, leaving the child, a young boy, standing pale and unprotected; but, possessed of unconscious skill as that of the bird that flies south in the winters of the ice-lands, he grasped the rocks with tiny, unblemished hands and clambered, shivering, on to the plateau that marked the northern end of the island. At once, as if following a path his young heart already knew, he turned and ran down the unbroken slab of stone that led to the island woods by the water's edge; then he was beneath the trees, walking on a twig-strewn avenue almost in darkness.

Soon the path became more tangled, and even he, small child as he was, was forced to stoop often between twisted briars

and branches of drooping thorn. And then, as he emerged from
a thicket of bramble and clumps of rushes half-buried in a
stagnant pool of water, he found himself in a clearing, completely empty of rock or tree, and deep in a pale grass that was
balm to his feet. Tempted for a moment to stay and rest there,
he hesitated; but then, as if recalling that he must go on, he
began almost at once to pad quietly over the grass at the edge
of the clearing, and was soon once more in the depths of the
forest.

Now he neared the western shore. Like an animal he stopped
often to ascertain whether the path he followed was true; then
he battled anew through the uncleared waste of tendrils and
thorns.

The moon went, faded in the last grey darkness before dawn.
Sometimes he slipped on a frost-covered stone, and fell forward
into the thorns; but he did not weep with the pain, and his
face was set ever more surely towards the west. Now the first
creatures were stirring, not disturbed by his passing but awakened by the first breaths of dawn and a new day. The trees too
stirred gently, and he looked up into the interwoven branches
high above, and smiled innocently, a naked child in a land of
danger and death of which he as yet knew nothing. And so he
came near to the shore, and heard the water lapping on the
wide beaches.

He found himself on the bank of a tongue of water that cut
into the island in a narrow inlet. Beyond, he saw the still, open
water which he instinctively knew he must reach, and beyond
it a grey shadow that rose up above the sea, forming an endless
shore. For a time the boy fought his way impatiently through
the uncleared undergrowth of the shore, eager now to win each
step towards his goal; but the tendrils and interwoven branches
were almost unyielding, and instead, determined to reach the
point where the open water began, he chose to wade out into
the freezing water and find his path there.

So at length he reached the point, shivering uncontrollably
in the growing wind, water streaming from his arms and
shoulders. The canopy of leaves above shimmered; speckled
shadows danced on the ripples; the trees on the island shore
behind him were locked together in an impenetrable dark wall.

And he had suffered for his courage; his limbs and chest were lined with thin trails of blood, the traces of tearing thorns and rough-leaved plants that had disfigured his young skin.

He looked up, over the water and the skein of silver mist that still covered the sea; and he felt the wind tugging at him, rising and falling over the island and forest, drying his body and freezing the moisture on it, for the sun had still not risen. The mist was curling away from the sea with the wind, so that now the far shore was becoming more clear as the light grew and the dawn sky became pure once more. And as he looked, he saw that a silent shadow was nosing gracefully through the water. A moment later a canoe was visible in the grey light, a paddle skimming the water, rising now to catch the first light, as drops like diamonds fell from the wood. Then he saw a woman's face. As she neared him, he noticed the plain white gown she wore. Their eyes met, and she smiled.

She came nearer, and then laid down the paddle in the craft and let the canoe glide in on the current. At the mouth of the inlet it stopped, and she beckoned to the child. 'Come', she said very softly. Yet the boy stood still on the shore, and seemed to hesitate; no voice could command him; he could only obey as his heart led him. She could easily have brought the canoe to the shore, taken it to the very point and held out her hand to him, but she did not. She was offering him a choice; and he had the power to obey, or to turn away and be lost. If he refused, no second chance would be possible.

In a moment he knew which way his heart led, and, stepping out, he moved without fear through the rippling waves; and again she smiled gently as he reached the craft, and lifted him in with strong arms. He sat still, enjoying the rocking motion of the canoe; still shivering, he yet noticed the slight warmth of the new day as the sun, now risen, began to filter through the trees.

Now the woman's paddle cut deep into the waves with a strong and effortless rhythm. The canoe left the shore of the island as quietly as it had come, the prow making a pathway of ripples like the golden head of an otter half-submerged beneath the waves. The mists were rolling away, drifting from the hills of the island; above, now, wide and empty, stretched a sky of pure azure.

'You are one of the Unborn', said the woman in her quiet sweet voice, which now had sadness in it. 'You must enjoy every moment of the beauty you see today, dear child, and hold it in your heart, for you do not have long before you must face a life of bitterness and slavery. You look at me with all the innocence of first youth. Ah, my little one, do I not pity all your race?' He saw that there were tears in her eyes.

For a while the canoe glided silently through the calm water; then the woman spoke again. 'How often have I wept for your brothers and sisters who have come with me upon this sea! And I have watched them leave, to walk through ice and snow as they approached the jaws of their hell, where the evil of the Voice, the one who holds them in thrall, awaits them. Ah, child, if I were still a Pyrian, and could read the prophecies of Celroc of old, then perhaps I could have hope of the long-awaited Fawn-leader, for such a one might come and master the Voice, and set our land free again! But I fear it is a vain hope, and my heart has been broken too often'. She stopped speaking, and the child went on looking at her uncomprehendingly, soothed a little all the same by the gentleness in her voice.

The channel between the island and the side shore of the mainland was shallow; a smooth bed of rock nestled a score of feet below the waves, and here, below the expanse of green fronds and leaves, it was deep still. The boy was quiet, looking intently down into the water. Then he turned to the land, and saw that it was bleak, covered by a rolling mist that moved ominously over the valleys, bringing a driving snow which came like needles of ice. He shivered again.

The woman seemed not to notice the cold; she whispered, as if to herself: 'He is not satisfied with what he has gained; he seeks nothing less than the utter destruction of a proud people, through pain and the slow, bitter death of defeat that has no end'. Then, seeming to notice the child again, she stooped and drew out from under her seat a woollen garment which she wrapped round him with the tenderness of a mother, letting the canoe for a moment twist and turn at the mercy of the waves. 'There, little one', she said in her soft voice. 'This, the one thing I can give to you to ease your suffering: wrap it tightly about you, for you will have great need of it'. As she spoke, there came with the snow a bitter and chilling wind which stirred the waves and ripples of the water into angry crests of foaming white.

At last they came into the lee of the mainland, where the waters were calmer; and the small craft glided beneath high cliffs, and the storm subsided and a pale light returned to the sky. Here, the way was dangerous; the channel before them had the grotesque appearance of the open mouth of a giant, with decayed rocks which seemed to leer at them as they passed. From the prow, the child leaned as if fascinated, searching the depths where shadows played eerily on the wave-crests; while above him the woman now stood, watchful and silent. Thus they passed on, and entered a different channel, free of the danger of rock-spars, where the woman guided the canoe past hummocks of reed-covered flats, and through a maze of small islands whose rushes swayed and rustled in the last winds of the storm. The prow now began to drive a path through the ice, and all the land was a dreary grey, with snow-covered islands and the frozen mud of the causeways that formed paths between them. And as the cold blue skies returned and the sun again began to shine free of the storm-clouds, the woman turned the canoe deftly into the last shallow waters of the channel, and let it come to rest among the reeds. With strong but gentle hands she lifted the pale child from the prow, and set him down on the firm ground, bending on one knee to say farewell, as she might to a king.

'Go now', she whispered, 'for I can lead you no further. My task is done. You yourself know your path, for it is written in your heart. All I ask is this one thing – do not allow the evil of the Voice to defeat you!' Then, taking the tiny hand in hers, she looked deep into the large, serious brown eyes. And then she turned, and, not looking back at him, she had taken up the paddle and without a sound had turned the craft from the reeds and was gone, the ripples dying behind her as she vanished behind the islands. The child did not hesitate for a moment; he realised that the bond was severed, and he turned away at once to find the path he must follow.

The icy wind had gone; light bathed the winter shores as he left the water to find his way over the rocky crest; now tongues of sparkling ice lay there like strange white snakes on the grass. Often he fell heavily, bruising himself again and again on the jagged spurs of rock. But he did not think of turning away from his destiny. He found at last an ice-filled gap between the rocks, and the path which many had followed before him. His punishment had begun on the very first day of his existence; cut and bruised, accepting and unquestioning, he stumbled on.

Beyond the ridge lay the land, west and south of him in endless plains, rugged and high above the sea, plains that rose up in the north, frozen into the Ice-Crests. About him, as he plodded over the rocky ground, the land lay in the grip of winter; between the hilly Strells, pools of silver water sparkled, locked in a fist of ice. All was dead, silent, devoid of life; only a thin wind rasped like eerie laughter over the endless wasteland. Throughout the long morning flurries of snow swept over the plains from the west, and ridges and banks of deep white grew and stretched like giant furrows across the table-land. Twice the boy fell, gasping and clutching the ice, hands raw and frozen; twice he rose and struggled on, mutely, his only comfort the woollen robe which the woman had given him, and which he wrapped more tightly round his small form as the blizzard increased in force. And always, without hesitation, he knew his path; obediently he took each step, though every time it led further into the open snare ahead, every time further from the hope of beauty and spring. At last the sun was vanquished, swallowed up in the utter greyness of the skies, and the land was dark. Noon, with the raging of the blizzard, might well have been midnight.

So ended the first day; and the boy slipped at last, spent, into a rocky chasm in whose lowest reaches a pale, grey stretch of frozen snow and ice loomed. His hands reached out and were buried as they fell, but he was beyond feeling their pain and lay there, his face upturned to the sky. He felt that he was being tortured by a power he could not comprehend; already all hope seemed to ebb away from him. And when, much later, the storm had finally passed and a myriad stars burned in the sky, he did not hear the sound of rocks and snow being dislodged behind him, nor did he awaken to see another child of his own kind fall gratefully asleep by his side.

Chapter 2

Childhood

He awoke as the last stars were fading above him in the narrow gap which had been his sanctuary. The cold was intense; his limbs seemed almost frozen after the night of storm and wind. The moon, a little past the full, still shone brightly and made the plains hauntingly clear. Drifts of frozen snow lay in the hollows as far as the eye could see; and never had there been such quietness, such absolute stillness, as in those moments before the stars and the moon were gone and the new dawn came. The little boy stood entranced, his ankles deep in a furrow of snow that had gathered in the wind, hardly daring to believe that the storm could be gone so soon. There was not a breath stirring; no creature moved, and the plains were still. So caught up was he in the beauty and peace after the cruelty of the storm that he did not yet sense the presence near him. Then, as dawn began to break, a shadow fluttered low above the plains, searching, beating curved wings. An owl perched on the topmost rock of the fissure, claws clutching the thin ice, unblinking golden eyes fixed on the child. For a moment its wings rose up round it and the spread of every feather and the glow of its eyes were caught and captured in the growing light. Suddenly the silence was broken, and the figure near the boy cried out in terror. In that moment the owl turned and, shrieking angrily, lifted moth-like from the chasm and was gone across the plains.

When the last raucous cries of the bird were lost in the silence, the boy turned to the intruder and their eyes met. He saw a little girl, no smaller or larger than himself, clutching around her a woollen garment which had clearly been given her by the woman in the canoe. In her eyes, as in his own, there was a sadness born of rejection. Though she looked now at the boy in shame, in the knowledge that he had witnessed and might mock her fear, she yet reached out to him, conscious already of the bond that joined her to him as one of her own people. And this was the paradox – the day-old innocence of their youth and the simple nature of their hearts that led them on this unknown and daunting way, and the communion of their souls in the awareness, deep down, of abandonment; the huddling together of their unprotected, unloved beings against the elements, against the future they had already learned to fear. They shared no words on that first strange meeting, nor would they through the days and troubles that lay ahead before they reached the end of their path; but a bond was forged between them, and the little girl forgot her shame as together they left the chasm and began to take the path they both instinctively recognised.

Night was now fully over, the gold and scarlet of the east dazzling and at last vanishing as the sun rose over the island and the sea. The tableland lay high above the cliffs, a battered, barren wasteland lying helpless in the fist of winter, and higher, as it rose in the north to close in the land in the Ice-Crests, unknown and frozen for all time. Their path crossed the plains for many miles before it dropped sharply down to the grass-lands, the Strells, and the warmer fields where the River Quenil wound sluggishly from the caves. Winter would be savage enough there, but here, high on the strange plains, it was awesome to even the most fearless. And these small children were stumbling over the snow-deep ground, without food or fire for their comfort; yet they possessed a strength to endure, a resilience, given to them by the perverse ruler of that land, who would have them suffer to the uttermost but not die. Now they were aware only of the path which led them onwards; and as they went on, the first grey storm-clouds grew heavy in the west and the wind began to blow fiercely.

Before them, all around, lay a strange and forbidding terrain. Large mounds of porous rocks lay everywhere; wreaths of snow and ice wound round them, filling every crevice and lining every fissure; snow fell thickly, blinding them as they battled on. On and on they stumbled, mile after mile. And then they found themselves walking in an avenue of giant monoliths, rugged pillars which loomed high above, unmistakable markers of the way they must take. The storm was now at its height, the wind screaming and moaning as if a thousand unearthly voices were locked in its frenzy. The cold was intense. The children were being led upwards, to a rough hilltop shrouded in the storm; each step they won, gasping, brought them to the next, on and on until the avenue broadened at last on the flat crown of the mound into a wide enclosure of stone. As the weary children reached this point the storm at last eased, and for a few moments, thankfully, they were able to rest.

When they at length went beyond the crest of the hill and found themselves descending into the mist-filled plains, they found their path mingled like a stream with the rocks. The boy was sometimes ahead, sensing the way unfalteringly, his feet half-buried in snow; sometimes, no less skilfully, the girl would step out and lead the way. And now, with the violence of the storm abated, the distant valleys of the Tremos and the Quenil could be seen, far below, in the warmer lands, where the Strells were also visible, pure and green, waiting for the breath of spring to awaken them. And then they were gone again, veiled from sight by the billowing mists.

At noon, as for a time the wind lulled over the drifted furrows of snow about the rocks, and the grey sky lifted to reveal the blue which had brightened the sunrise, they came down wearily to a close wall of pines across their path. Silently they passed between the boughs into the dusky stillness of a forest, the shed needles of past years sharp to their feet, and the first sunlight since dawn gleaming between the canopy of branches. They felt strangely comforted by the presence of the trees. Each chose a different way, the girl walking ahead, their feet making no sound on the forest floor, until behind them the trees closed into darkness. Here was no snow to bury the feet, no storm battering against their frail forms, only the stirring and distant murmuring of long-frozen branches as the wind passed, high above, in the canopy of the trees.

At length they came from the stillness of the pines to a place where the ground was covered with undisturbed snow; and as the eye searched deeper into the valley, meadows of green lay still and lush, untroubled by the clasp of winter, with the blue thread that was the Quenil passing into the Grass Strells between. The children paused just long enough to notice that the storm was gone, and with it the insufferable chill of the higher plains; leaving the plateau and the pines behind, they descended into the valley. Here at their feet was the source of the river, the stream chuckling and frothing down the slopes to settle into the long, devious course that wound and wove its way among the Strells and south to the sea. In winter much of its surface was dense with ice, strong enough to allow herds of wandering deer to cross timorously in search of food; but when the spring days returned, its course was turned into a churning, grey spate, filled with the melted snow of the tablelands.

They met the first ice-covered pools of the stream as they stepped down into the steep ravine that stretched jaggedly into the west and held the course of the Quenil. The boy advanced first among the jutting rocks at the edge of the gorge where the first grass grew, and then he was gone, down swiftly into the perilous descent that led to the valley, the stream gushing at his back like a silver plume. The roar of the spouting water was loud in his ears as he found his path with difficulty on the steep scree slope, the mass of shale and ice subsiding beneath his feet and carrying him helplessly downwards. Above him, as he looked back at last, he saw the girl standing by the falls: she seemed to hesitate for a moment, and then she too was launched on the descent and soon had landed among the debris beside him, panting a little but triumphant.

The Quenil was a faithful guide for a time, before its course took it away in a great westward sweep; and by afternoon, as the dusk began to deepen, they heard again its welcome babble. A river it was now, swelled by the streams of the northern plains and full already with the melted snows that heralded the first days of spring. The children picked their way between the rocks and drank deeply from the ice-cool water. Yet, tempted as they were to rest there, they pressed on; tired as their bodies were, their hearts urged them onwards. Soon the sound of the river was lost as their path turned south by the looming walls of the ravine.

It was fully night when they came, footsore and utterly spent, to the great cave-mouth where they knew they must find their passage. The moon was up now and as, in silence, they looked back for a moment, the wide plains behind them lay silver in its brilliance. There lay the beauty of a land they were destined never to know; and in darkness they turned to enter the jaws of the caves where darkness indeed awaited them.

Echoes seemed to call eerily from the black emptiness of the passage. For the first time, the girl came close to the boy and, in silence, sought his hand; they went on together. Streams gurgled and shone wickedly from crumbled cavities in the stone wall. They passed a yawning chasm in the floor, the rock-face falling away into emptiness. The echoes of dislodged stones came much later, dull murmurings in the depths of the mountain, and when all was still again, suddenly a sound like demented laughter resounded all around them. Fear gripped their hearts, but they went on resolutely.

They descended countless passages and passed more vast caverns than any mountain might have been thought to contain; yet at length the sounds which they had been hearing for some time became voices, and their path brought them to caves in which people dwelt. Suddenly, torchlight flickered sickly against their faces, shadows passed over visages of unbelievable gauntness, over eyes half hidden by wild, unkempt hair, over sunken souls whose faces showed clearly their hopelessness. They seemed to freeze as the children entered; with unblinking eyes they stared at them, yet made no sound; their gaze followed them as they passed through into the grey gloom of the passages beyond.

The boy and girl did not linger; they knew this was not yet the end of their journey, and they must keep on. So they passed cave after cave with their unsmiling, staring inhabitants, tribe after tribe of ragged, wild-miened folk; and then at last they entered side by side a low-roofed cavern whose walls were bright with the glow of lighted brands. One by one, as in the far dimness the noise and confusion died away, each villager looked around and saw them and was still. Sharply a woman scolded a young boy; then silence fell. The children now stood, knowing their journey ended. An old man came forward, extending emaciated arms in the only welcome he could give.

His face was serious, but his eyes smiled at the orphans. 'Come, children', he said in a gentle voice. 'Do not be afraid. We welcome you. Come and live among us, and we will share with you the little that we have; for we are the Unborn, your own people'.

Chapter 3

The Caves of Half-life

So began for the children a time of darkness, a time unmarked by summers or winters, unrelieved by glimpses of sun or moon or stars; a time of perpetual hardship, when hunger continually stalked among the doomed inhabitants of the caves.

And yet, among the people whose lives the children had come to share, there was no lack of kindness or even of love. The boy, on that first day, was welcomed in the arms of a woman who had received him as tenderly as a mother. His strength had been so drained by the toil of the winter march that he did not question the love which she, half fearfully, offered him; he slept almost at once, and lay in her arms for many hours, wakening to see bending over him a twisted face and body, but one with a look of such gentleness that he knew no fear. Her name was Maria. By some she was shunned because of her disfigurement; she had known this always, and saw the confusion in the eyes which turned away from her. The pain of her tortured body kept her sleepless for long hours by the last embers of the midnight fire. She did not seek the compassion of others, and hers had been a lonely life till the boy came.

She called him Ivan. He never called her mother, nor did she ask him to; it was enough that she was allowed to care for him, to guard him and make clothes and rough shoes for his feet. But as the slow years went on, there grew between the two a bond of love.

The tall old man, called Peter, a leader among the cave people and the one who had held out hands of welcome to the children, was the one into whose special care the girl had come. As she grew, she learned to love and respect this man who at all times worked for the good of the rejected ones who were his own people, the Unborn. As time passed and Kerry, the young girl, grew in understanding, she began to know something of the sadness and fear which were the lot of all who lived in the caves. But for the children there was at times some childish joy; they played together, learned to talk and run and laugh, and to share the pathetic toys made out of animal bones which were the only playthings they knew. There were many children in the nearby caves; yet from the first day the bond forged between the boy and the girl held fast, and they would sit for long hours at peace together; and together, hand in hand, they explored the secrets of the labyrinth of caves, and found a place of solace near the sunken lake from which the villages drew their water.

Time passed, and little by little the growing boy and girl learned more of the cruel ruler of the land who held the Unborn in thrall. For Ivan, the knowledge first came from Maria. He had returned to her at the end of the day, and after she had shared with him her meagre repast, they sat together by the dying embers of the fire, a brand burning fitfully above their heads. The boy looked with compassion at the contorted features of his guardian and friend. 'Why are you always so sad, Maria?' he asked softly.

'Child', she answered, 'do you not know the Voice, the wicked one who holds us here and whispers to us at nights the things that break our hearts?'

'I have heard him', replied the boy, 'only once or twice. He tells me there is no hope for us'. She stroked the soft hair and held him close. But that night she said no more.

Like a father, Peter watched the girl Kerry grow, seeing her budding beauty, seeing too in her the first clouding of her childhood days by fear and hopelessness. At last he spoke to her of the desolation which was the lot of all the Unborn, and of the cruel whispering Voice. Already, she told him, she knew this Voice; often in the night her sleep was spoiled by this invisible being who whispered over and over, so that she had no rest or peace. With great sadness, Peter told her what she must know.

'My poor girl', he said with infinite kindness, 'my poor Kerry, you will come to understand more and more as time goes on of this evil one who speaks to us all, who torments us and takes away all our hope. He speaks to some to drive them to madness. We are here, underground, because of him; and not we alone in this village, but many villages full of trapped, unhappy souls, men, women and children like ourselves throughout these catacombs in the mountains, all because of the Voice, and the fear he has put on us of ever trying to leave here. The Priests are his servants. Whenever they came in the past, when you were younger, we took care that you did not remain here where we live, but were far away in the caves where the children play; but now it is right that you should know the truth. When the wicked Priests come, always at the time of the full moon, they take away one person from one of the villages. These unfortunate ones they lead away, never to be seen again; but we know they are taken to be killed, and afterwards their spirits go to the kingdom of the Voice himself, there to serve him as tormented souls. We are powerless to help them.'

Peter bowed his head in grief; he did not speak again for a long time, while Kerry sat motionless. 'All this is hard for you to bear, my Kerry,' he said at last. 'Would that I had never had to tell you! But you must know, for you too are one of the Unborn, and our fate is also yours. But do not let fear destroy you! Never let hope be lost. Sleep now, my child, and try as much as you can to forget'.

She did sleep, but her rest seemed to be filled with foreboding, and wild dreams made her restless night after night. Winter came, more cruel that year than ever, and hunger was a daily enemy to be feared: there was no laughter left in the faces of the people she met, but in some a quiet determination to fight against darkness and death. Yet as the days passed resolve seemed to grow less, and for some a kind of frenzy took its place. Food became ever more scarce. The cold was intense, and wasted forms huddled round the fires at night. And the whisperings of the Voice filtered into every heart, whispering despair and death; children rose up wailing in their sleep; like pale ghosts they wandered terrified to escape their tormentor, until they were found and comforted against the darkness. The fear grew daily more tangible; and as Kerry lay awake in the pale glow of the brand burning above her, she saw that Peter turned again and again in his sleep, and once she thought his lips fought to mutter 'No, no!' In the morning he seemed uneasy and spoke little; yet if anything she felt his compassion had increased, and the sadness and love in his eyes intensified. He could not bear the weeping of the children, and gave up his own meagre ration for a wild-eyed boy whose body was shrivelled with hunger.

It was about this time that, one night when Ivan could not sleep and as always Maria sat hunched over the dying fire, the boy heard something of his guardian's story and understood why she was so often sunk in gloom. 'Maria', he asked hesitantly, 'What do you know . . . what has the Voice said to you?'

She looked up, startled. After a pause, she replied slowly: 'He tells us all that there is no hope for us, over and over again'.

'Yes, I know that', he went on, 'but to you, Maria, what does he say to you of why you came to be one of the Unborn?'

The woman hesitated again for what seemed a long time. Then in an almost inaudible voice she said: 'Dear boy, almost a son to me, why should I not tell you, although I have told nobody else? You are closer to me than any other; never have you turned away from my poor face and my twisted body. You know of course,' she continued, 'that the evil one tells us things only to drive us to despair, and for no other reason. Over the years he has told me everything that could make me sad – all that might have been, to bring torment to my poor heart. My parents were good, gentle people. They were ageing, and had long wished for a child to cheer their lives; when they knew that my mother was to bear a child at last, their joy knew no bounds. And then the blow fell. When they were told that I would be born like this' – she faltered for a moment – 'I became a threat, a terror to their minds. My mother wept long, refusing to be comforted; she suffered much before she would agree to my destruction. But my father, although he was a good man, was proud; he could not have endured the shame of a child who would disgrace his name. All this I have learned from the one who keeps us prisoners here. He tells us these things to drive us to despair', she repeated. 'And to add to the sadness of the lot that might have been mine, he has told me too that had my parents only been brave enough to let me live, despite my poor maimed body I would have given them much happiness and peace! As it was, they died in sadness and loneliness.'

The boy sat in silence, then came to kneel beside Maria with his arm close about her. Much later he slept, but his sleep was troubled, and twice she heard him cry out.

Time went on, and both Ivan and Kerry grew, and left behind childish games, and became part of those who worked to provide for the children and the old and infirm in their village. More and more they became aware of the deep fears which plagued their people. Above all, the recurrent nightmare of the possibility that their village might provide the Priests' next victim was with them all. One night an old woman near Kerry had risen demented in her sleep, crying 'They're coming! I've seen the Voice! I'm going to die!' And as the girl in terror got up and searched her face, she had sagged back exhausted and said no more. Kerry slept no more that night; next day, in their secret place, she had told Ivan of the incident and as always he had comforted her. Their friendship was to both the greatest solace of all.

The other fear present at all times was that of hunger. One day, to their great sadness, they found that, far along in the labyrinth of caves, fighting had broken out over some deer which had strayed into one of the villages. Word had spread fast, and more and more starving people had joined in the battle, some tearing at the raw flesh in their lust for meat. At night, Kerry had helped Peter bathe and bind up the wounds of those of their own tribe who had fought over the carcases. Never had she seen the old man so sad: he had suffered to see men, women and especially children ever more gaunt with hunger; even more, it seemed, did he hate to see them fight with others of their own kind who knew the same misery. 'Peace!', he said quietly to those whom he now tended, 'what hope is there for us, my people, if we cannot learn to live in peace?'

Soon after this, the final blow fell for Kerry. For some time she had been growing ever more anxious about Peter, the old man who was to her the symbol of all that made the hard life of the caves bearable – Peter the strong, the leader, the one who watched over his people with unending devotion, who shared his own food with the children, the one to whom all turned instinctively when in fear or doubt. But to Kerry, especially, the one who embodied all she knew of the love of a father. Now he seemed increasingly to shrink into himself; for long hours he would sit motionless, staring into the fire. And one night, when she lay awake late and heard him toss and turn in the darkness, he suddenly cried out 'No, no! I cannot leave them!' That night she slept only fitfully. She resolved that at all costs she must find out what it was that troubled him so deeply; in the morning she would demand that he share his burden with her, now that she was grown and could understand.

So, whenever the old man had begun to build their fire next day, Kerry faced him with her need to know. For a time he answered nothing, but finally, sighing deeply, he replied: 'You are right, my dear child; you must know, and it is only my cowardice that has prevented me from telling you. But you must be brave, my Kerry, for my words will cause you sadness. Soon I am to leave you: I am destined to be a victim of the Voice, and his Priests will come for me'.

For a moment the girl was stunned; then, rushing to him with her arms wide, she cried out 'No, Peter, no! Not you, of all people! We cannot do without you! Surely you must be mistaken? And who said . . . how do you know?' She began to sob bitterly.

Peter held her gently, and said quietly, 'Dear one, we always know. The Voice tells us, long in advance, so that each of us may suffer to the full. I have heard him whisper these tidings to me for a long time now. And although he is evil, in this at least he speaks the truth. They will come for me soon'. He held her in silence then until her grief subsided. 'I know I can trust you to be strong, Kerry, for the sake of the others', he said at last. 'And I know too that you will do all that I have taught you. And never forget this – your coming brought me great joy in my last years. Now go, dear girl. I must be alone for a time'.

Her first thought was to share her grief with Ivan. She rushed to find him, and requested of Maria that they might go for a little to their old childhood haunt by the underground lake. The

woman smiled and assented; she too was fond of Kerry, and
accepted the bond between the two. Ivan had at once noticed
the signs of recent tears, and could not wait to hear the cause
of her distress. 'What is wrong, Kerry?' he asked anxiously; but
she would not speak until they had reached the place where so
often in past years they had shared their secrets. Then she burst
out in wild weeping; he held her close, whispering words of
comfort and waiting until she should be able to tell him what
was wrong. At last the terrible words were out; Ivan, shocked
and incredulous, repeated the girl's own words to Peter: 'It
cannot be . . . what should we do without him? Surely he must
be mistaken!' Gently, she in turn explained that Peter had
known for a long time – it was always thus.

Filled with sorrow and foreboding, their thoughts in turmoil,
they sat silent for a time. As on the far-away day of their first
journey, they huddled together for comfort; they, the abandoned ones who had known rejection for all of their short lives,
knew that their only hope lay in each other. They might have
stayed all day, but the boy remembered that Maria had been ill
and needed him. In silence they returned. All that night the
Voice tormented Ivan; in vain he held his hands tight to his
ears; still the hated whisper taunted him, filling him with frenzy
and hopelessness. Then, near the morning, he left him. And
in that moment, desperate, the boy knew that he must leave
the caves, and, whatever the cost, go and find the hated tormentor and destroy him. But how? Had anyone ever escaped from
this place of torture before? Surely not; or if they had, they
must surely have perished. Who could hope to stand against
this evil power? And what of Kerry? How could he possibly
leave his closest friend? And Maria, who was as a mother to
him?

For days he kept these thoughts to himself, but they seemed
to burn in his soul. And each night the Voice, knowing his
rebellion, whispered ceaselessly to torment him. 'Fool', the
hated one ranted in his ears, 'know that nobody, nobody, has
ever escaped from my prison, least of all a puny weakling like
you'. At times the boy would feel all his resolve ebbing away; he
would know it was hopeless, hopeless . . . but in the morning,

whenever he had peace from the torment, resolution would again rise in him.

At last he determined to tell Kerry. Whatever she thought, she would not mock him; although parting would be hard, unthinkably hard, for them both, she would be bound to feel as he did that at all costs an attempt must be made to overcome the unbearable evil under which all of the Unborn laboured. Yet despite his assurance of her understanding, it took him several days to find the courage to tell her. When at last he did, her response overwhelmed him – she too had come to a firm decision; If Peter were to be taken, as sadly it seemed certain he would be, then no matter what it cost (and she felt sure it would mean death for both of them) both she and Ivan must go, together, and in some way seek to destroy the Voice. She had been trying for days to find words in which to share her resolve with him, but had held back because of one great obstacle – Maria.

Maria! She had been constantly in Ivan's thoughts. She had lately been ill a great deal, which made the thought of abandoning her even harder. 'I know, Kerry,' Ivan said with a note of desperation. 'I have battled with the thought of her hour after hour. Even the Voice taunts me with this – she has been my guardian, and it would kill her if I left!' He bent his head and covered his face with his hands. Kerry was silent in sympathy for a time. At last he stood up, as if with a new resolve. 'It has to be done,' he said quietly. 'We'll go and tell her at once, together. She has great strength, despite her frail body, and she will understand. Whatever happens, we can face it together!'

Hand in hand, they made their way back towards the caves. Whenever the time came to leave, they would be ready.

Chapter 4

Peter

A strange sound assailed their ears as their steps drew near to the caves of their own village, a kind of eerie chant, mixed with the wailing of women. Their hearts stood still; both instinctively recognised that the thing they most dreaded had come to pass. It was the Priests, come to claim the latest victim of the cruel Voice. For a moment they stopped, their bodies as if turned to ice. Then Kerry cried out in a voice of utter desolation, 'Peter! Oh, they have come for Peter!' Suddenly she began to run, hopelessly, knowing in her heart what she would find; stumbling, blinded by tears, terrified, Ivan followed at her heels, no less filled with foreboding, hearing the dread chanting coming nearer, with now and then a woman's scream of pure despair. They reached the old man's cavern and stopped dead in silence; the Priests were there, already bearing Peter aloft, and ready to move away on their journey. For the moment, the dread chant had ceased.

They stood like ghostly shadows in the entrance of the cave, their faces pale, whiter almost than the sweeping robes that adorned them. Their eyes burned with absolute malevolence, the evil mockery of the Voice, their master; three unblinking owls – symbols of their priesthood – rested on their shoulders. The huge brands they carried shed gouts of golden flame, making the light in the cavern seem sickly in comparison. The heads of all the people around were bowed; all was for a moment silent. Then Kerry rushed forward, crying 'Peter! Oh, Peter, my dear father!' Before anyone could stop her, she had reached up to embrace the old man. Roughly one of the Priests pushed her away; she fell awkwardly to the ground, Ivan rushing to comfort her.

'Fools!' cried a Priest in a raucous voice of pure hatred. And then turning to Kerry, he added, 'Do not dare to touch him, or you too will go on a journey with us!'

Suddenly a quiet, steady voice interrupted. It was Peter, deathly pale but calm. 'Goodbye, beloved Kerry', he said. 'Try not to grieve for me, and remember all I taught you. Care for the weak always!'

'Come then, old man', snarled another of the Priests, 'you have spent long enough already on your touching valediction!' He laughed mockingly. 'The path your brothers and sisters have trodden before you awaits you!' Slowly the procession moved away.

Ivan, desperate to say even a word of farewell, found himself unable to speak; yet curiously he felt it was he, rather than the old man, who was in need of comfort. He turned instead to comfort Kerry, who had shrunk back into the darkness of the cave where the light from the brands could not reveal her anguish. Demented laughter echoed through the passages beyond, marking the departure of the Priests; then the awful sounds receded and they were alone.

At once the girl started up. 'Ivan!' she cried, 'we must follow! There's not a moment to lose! Please, go now and tell Maria, while I get ready'. He agreed without demur, indeed there was no time to lose. But as he left, he thought with a sinking heart of the interview ahead; he would not even have Kerry's support when he told Maria of their plans. Yet there was no possible choice; and despite his dread of telling her, he still trusted Maria to be courageous.

And he had not misjudged her. At once she understood; though tears stood in her eyes, and later she would weep much, she drew on the reserve of strength built up over long years of loneliness and darkness; knowing the cost to the boy, seeing indeed the anguish in his face, she at once resolved not only to let him go, but to release him from any sense of guilt in leaving her. 'Dear son,' she said in a quiet but steady voice, 'for that is what you have always been to me, there is no doubt in my mind about your going. Go with my blessing.' Her voice faltered for a moment, but at once she went on. 'It has been in my mind for a long time that you might become a leader among our people once Peter had gone. I had not thought he would go in this way' – a shudder passed through her frame – 'but even without this latest evil, is it not clear that someone has to make the attempt to defeat the one who holds all our people in fear?'

She could say no more. There was silence, and Ivan held her wasted form for a time; he could find no more words. It was Maria who broke the silence. Drawing on her strength once more, she said, 'Ivan, dearest, I am ill and I have not long to go. . . . thank you, thank you.' Choked, she could not go on.

The boy quickly packed a few meagre provisions, then gazed with a long look of pure love on the disfigured face; she held on to his hand a last time, a brief memory which would outlast all the bitterness of the sojourn in the land of darkness. He longed to pour out words of thanks, but none came. It fell to Maria to say the final words. 'Leave this hell and fight for all your people! Remember, what you do is for all the Unborn – we have no other hope but you.'

He turned at once and left the cave without a backward glance. He made his way directly to Peter's dwelling, expecting to find Kerry awaiting him impatiently; to his surprise and concern, she was nowhere to be seen. Where could she have gone? Surely she must realise how little time they had; already the Priests were well ahead of them. He went from cave to cave, searching anxiously, and then he saw her. She was bending over an old man who was clearly very ill, bathing his forehead with great tenderness. For a moment he felt anger sweep over him; how could she waste precious time in this way? 'What is this, Kerry? Have you forgotten so soon what we planned?' He scarcely recognised his own voice, so harsh did it sound.

She looked up then, with a face so anguished that he felt a stab of remorse; but he did not speak. 'Do not think I have forgotten Peter!' Kerry cried out after a moment. 'I am longing to leave, longing perhaps even more than you. But this poor man, a friend of Peter's, has been ill now for many days; he was wounded in the fight over the animals, and then he took a fever, and Peter knew he was dying and made me promise that I would nurse him at the end. And now he is near to death, and I cannot leave him! I feel sure he has at most a few hours to live'.

Then, all anger gone now, Ivan knelt beside her and looked intently at the dying man. He knew she was right; knew too that what she did was indeed what Peter would have her do, what he had instilled into her through all the years of her childhood. Had not his last words been 'care for the weak always'? But what were they to do? Should he perhaps leave her, and face the journey alone? His heart recoiled from the thought; yet if he must, he would. He called Kerry over to the shadows. Quietly he shared his thoughts with her. 'No, Ivan', she said with complete conviction. 'In a few short hours I shall be free. The determination to face the Voice for the sake of the Unborn came to each of us separately. This task is for me also'.

Ivan, realising the truth of her words, felt a wave of relief; even if they were destined to perish, how much better to be together! For a moment, remembering his last sight of Maria, his thoughts wandered. How touching had been her faith in him; how simple and strong her certainty that he could win through, that through his own and Kerry's sacrifice the Unborn could be redeemed, that the beauty of the land which lay above these mountains could one day be theirs! But Kerry was speaking again; he should have some sleep, she urged him; he would need all his strength for the journey ahead, and she too would snatch some rest even as she watched over the sick man. At last he wrapped himself in his cloak and lay down thankfully. Immediately he was assaulted by a torrent of abuse from the Voice; it was as if a stream of pure venom was engulfing him. He tossed and turned, vainly endeavouring to shut out the hateful whispers, the scornful threats of fearful punishment which all but caused him to run to Kerry and tell her it was all an impossible dream, and that they had better renounce all thought of a task so utterly beyond their strength. Then the Voice was quiet, and he passed into a fitful slumber in which he fought against monstrous beasts, and the ghostly faces of the Priests wavered before his eyes, and the owls left their shoulders and came at him with raucous cries. Then Kerry was bending over him, shaking him gently, and he awoke with relief; she was telling him that Jonathan had died, and she was ready to leave at once.

He arose and drank some water, found his provisions and was ready. He stopped for just a moment and looked back towards the cave where Maria doubtless lay awake in the darkness, and said softly, 'Goodbye, dearest Maria! We shall try not to fail you.' And then they were on their way at last, passing through cave after cave where wretched, hungry people lay finding solace in sleep, such solace indeed as was theirs when the frenzied whisperings left them in peace. Now and then a man or woman started up, or a child cried; but they were not assailed as they went silently on, hand in hand, pausing only for a moment to say farewell to the place by the sunken lake in which they had shared the secrets of childhood and had given to each other what little joy they had known.

But they must hurry – they had already lost so much precious time. Where would the Priests be now? The ghost of the moon would be fading with the coming of dawn, yet they would long since have left with their prisoner, and begun their march to the place of death, the rock of sacrifice. Now strange unearthly sounds seemed to echo around them as they hurried along, stumbling often on the uneven path; the caverns loomed emptily around them as they left behind the places of habitation; drops of stagnant water oozed from the ceilings. Inwardly, both found themselves now striving against the venomous whispers of the Voice; neither said a word. On and on they plodded, on for what began to seem like an eternity; it was impossible to imagine that they would ever win free, ever rise towards the light of an unfettered world.

At last there was a roaring in their ears which became ever louder; suddenly they saw a waterfall spouting from high in the walls of a vast cavern. As they came near, they were drenched with freezing spray. Its channel cut right across their path, and they saw that there could be no way round. Its span was many feet; the bed of the stream had been worn deep in the stone, and if a foot were to slip in the crossing, the traveller would soon be swept away. But there could be no turning back now. 'I'll jump first, Kerry, and then I'll help you over', shouted Ivan against the roar. In a moment he had leapt the chasm;

although her heart failed her, the girl did not hesitate and a moment later she too had jumped; he caught her, and she landed safe by his side.

Now the river was behind them; the darkness was before. Wearily they left the roaring turbulence of the falls and turned away into a new passage, low and dim, whose stony path wound onwards until the blackness swallowed it up. They were beyond talk now, so had the weariness and despair vanquished the small flame of hope in their hearts. The world is darkness now, whispered the Voice; the world has always been darkness for the Unborn. There is no way out; there never will be a way out. It is useless, useless, useless. The Unborn can never win. Feeling the pain of every step now on the hard stone, Kerry found she had forgotten why she had ever left her village. Both found their wills beginning to be dominated by the evil whisperings; to both came an ever-increasing temptation to turn back. 'Kerry', said Ivan slowly – and it seemed to her that his voice had become heavy and dull – 'Kerry', he whispered again, 'I am so tired! Could we not go back a little and sleep in the caves? Maybe there really is no way out, except for the Priests?'

She felt strongly tempted to agree, to turn back there and then, to find a place where they could sleep and sleep, where all struggle would be ended; but still the faint memory of some purpose lingered behind all her doubt and weakness, above all the seductive whisperings of the Voice. She stumbled and slid wearily over the rocks of the passage, her eyes almost closed in sleep. And then in her mind she seemed to hear another voice, one which urged her to resist the temptation to turn back. Then she found her feet taking her upwards over the rocks, to the left and afterwards to the right, into the darkness of the passage, until at last, still fighting against the enchantment, she looked up and half-opened her sleep-filled eyes. What she saw first was a kind of greyness, a strange half light that lay beyond the blackness of the walls; and for a time she simply stared at it listlessly, neither understanding nor caring. Then she pushed herself onwards again with short, weary steps, stopped for a time as she was briefly conquered by the sorcery, and seemed almost to fall asleep for a few moments.

When she again roused herself, she saw with surprise a thin

rim of pale gold tingeing the grey wall, and this time she forced
herself to open her eyes wide to its light. Memory flooded back
of the first dusk she had seen in that land of winter. Tiny child
though she had been, it was imprinted on her memory; how
could she have forgotten that last day of freedom? At last a stab
of pure joy pierced her imprisoned heart. She ran higher, free
at last of the grip of the Voice, weeping, stumbling through the
last shingle slopes of the tunnel, running towards the light.

It was not a dream! 'Ivan! Ivan!', she called back to him, her
voice no longer weak with grief and self-pity. On the crest of
the screes she spun round and saw, blurred through her tears,
his shadow and then his face, empty and spent, looking at her
uncomprehendingly. 'Ivan, don't you see, we're free!' she called
again. 'We have found the land above; it wasn't a dream! I can
see the mountains! Oh, it's so beautiful!' It was as if her voice
shattered the last shackles of that other, most hated Voice.

Suddenly he began to run after her, falling and laughing, up
at last on to the plains, those plains of which he had dreamed
for so long, and into the light denied him through the years.

She held out her arms to him as he reached her, but his eyes
could only take in what lay before and all around – the grass,
the skies, the mountains. Together they rested, drinking in the
beauty. Suddenly, as she gazed at the moon, the memory of
Peter flooded back to her, and it seemed all at once that its
brightness was occluded by a grey cloud of foreboding.

'Oh, Ivan!' she cried out in distress, 'I had forgotten Peter!
Look, do you not see the full moon? It may already be too late,
and I have failed him!' Overcome, she turned away, unable to
bear any more the glory of the moon; but Ivan rebuked her.

'No, Kerry, you have not failed him – you were the one who
kept on, when I was ready to turn you aside, to return to our
prison! You were the one who found the way!' He came to her
side and made her face him, and his voice was very gentle and
full of tenderness. 'No, it is I who should ask you to forgive
me my weakness. You withstood the evil seduction of the Voice
when I had been overcome. Don't you see, Kerry? He has been
fighting us all the way! It was his last chance to stop us before
we were free and found the true land; he tried to make us
forget our purpose in leaving the caves, tried to make us believe

it was all hopeless folly. But you did not forget; and now you have not forgotten Peter, and there may still be time, still a little time'.

She looked up at him gratefully, content to be quiet for a moment. They stood on the wide, snow-swept plains, still drinking in the beauty denied to them for so long, and slowly realising that somehow the terrible domination of the Voice had been left behind. Ahead, they knew, must lie much danger, and doubtless suffering for them both; but with the light of the full moon making the world seem almost as bright as day, they could not deny the strong hope which was beginning to well up in their hearts.

Chapter 5

The Rock of Sacrifice

Ivan was not long in pointing out to Kerry the goal they sought. The great mound of black rock was unmistakable; it rose up dramatically from the plains round about, which seemed to stretch away endlessly. Kerry shuddered as she looked at it – to think that it was Peter himself who had told them this was where the victims of the Priests were killed! Even as a wave of horror swept over her at the recollection, she found that sleep was conquering her resolve. She *must* rest, even for an hour, or she could not go on. She lay down, shivering, among the rocks, wrapping her heavy woollen cloak tightly around her, and almost immediately was asleep. Ivan for a time fought his own tiredness; he struggled to keep awake, searching the horizon anxiously for any sign of life. At last he too lay down and fell into a light and troubled sleep.

They awoke together, blinded by icy needles of snow. Now the moon was gone, blanketed and obscured by the blizzard; they would have to be guided by their memories of the terrain as they had seen it before they slept. Both were keenly aware that they had already wasted too much time. From now on, no matter how weary they might feel, there could be no more rest. And so they quickly left the shelter of the high rocks to step out into the shrieking violence of the storm. Snow swept in clouds before their faces; their eyes were blinded by spicules of ice which battered them mercilessly. Gasping, they bent forward, bowed with the pain of their every step, their benumbed hands joined for fear that in the vehemence of the wind they might be separated for ever. They faced, as far as they were able, into the emptiness of the plains to the south, towards the sinister mound of stone. Kerry, her eyes on the ground, could only fight to keep stumbling on in her companion's footprints. There was no escaping the torture of the icy snow; it beat against her face, numbing her senses. No rest was possible; the empty plains seemed to stretch onwards for an eternity. At last the blizzard eased and the moon shone eerily through the veil of the storm-clouds, but its light was like some weakly burning brand and could offer little comfort for their way.

Suddenly Ivan cried out sharply, and a moment later he had stopped and was searching for something which his foot had struck. She was too weak to make the effort to shout and ask what it was, but he reached again for her hand and led her on. All at once she found the violence of the wind lessening, and then the incessant buffeting of the snow had ceased; instead she became conscious of her own laboured breathing. Ivan led her into the narrow chasm of an overhanging rock, and there without a word they rested in the merciful silence. If only, she thought, we could stay here until the raging storm was over; what solace and peace were here.

'Can we not stay till the storm is over?', she said at last, despising herself for the petulant tone of her voice. 'It will surely be easier to find Peter then?', she continued; the thought of rest was so overwhelmingly desirable, and she doubted greatly whether she had the strength to go on. She sat down in utter weariness. Then Ivan turned and smiled gently at her: suddenly she was aware of the tiredness in his own eyes, and remembered that it had been he who had all the time beaten their path - how weary he too must be! He said no word of rebuke.

'I would dearly love to stay here, Kerry', he answered. 'I am frightened by this storm, frightened above all that we might be separated; but you know that the full moon will be gone by morning and Peter will be dead. We have got to find him before it is too late'. In his eyes she could see compassion for her weariness. 'Come, my dear, eat something', he went on gently. 'You will feel stronger then'.

In spite of herself she smiled at him, rubbing her frozen hands and then taking up the bread he held out to her, and drinking from the skin of water he had brought. The chill of the water seemed to revive her, and she was able to follow him to the edge of the chasm where, gasping, she felt again the onslaught of the wind and snow.

On they went again for what seemed like hour after endless hour, facing the fury of the wind, stumbling often, sometimes falling in the snow; each time Kerry would wish that she might be allowed to rest there and sleep for ever. Each time Ivan would be there to lift her, and on they would plod again. It seemed to her at last that there never had been a time without this merciless snow battering against her face, that winter had always been, that there could be no end.

Yet at last there came a blessed time when there were no more icy clouds sweeping over the plains, but instead a deathly stillness which was balm to their weary spirits. And then the moon came through the last veils of cloud, shining with such brilliance as to make each shadow precise, each far mountain as easily visible as by day. The tired travellers stopped and looked at the dazzling scene in pure wonder. The whole world had been turned to silver. They stood there while only a breath of wind now sighed from the north, and the last lonely flakes of snow were lit by the shining moon – a picture of beauty, peace, and freedom. As their hearts lifted, they were both aware of a new energy; as if their deliverance from the pain of the storm had revived their flagging spirits, they began simultaneously to run, he racing ahead of her and sliding down each little slope, she laughing as she chased after him over the snow. For the moment it was as if they had been released from the distress of their mission. They ran side by side at last, more slowly now since the cold was so intense, but happy to be near each other, relishing the silence of the plains.

All at once they saw looming above them, like a square chiselled pillar of stone, what they had come all this way to find. The moonlight made its surface strangely bright, showed the wide cracks and crevices that split its buttresses and high, smooth walls; it shone on the narrow, perilous ledges that ran along its sides. Below it, nearer to them now, as they stopped breathless at last, flowed the ice-thick Poleria, the river that came winding through the plains, and whose waters were buried now beneath the winter load of snow and ice. The silence of night was oppressive, giving the impression to the travellers that it had always been like this – always silence, always winter.

So they went on, nearer and nearer to the shadow of the great rock that jutted from the plain, abandoned perhaps by some primeval flow of ice. Ivan's eyes were already searching its walls as he stepped down from the high bank into the hollow channel of the river. Somehow a path had to be found on that shimmering pillar of stone, if Peter were by any means to be reached before the full moon had gone. After that, he would be dead; and morning could not now be far away.

The ice, as they crossed the river, sometimes splintered into a thousand fragments beneath their feet; sometimes the water bubbled up through the frozen snow. Ivan held Kerry's hand tightly as together they slid over the uneven ice, step by step with the greatest of care; then they were safe, and clambering up on the far bank. Suddenly the towering rock seemed much nearer, and soon they were in its dark shadow. The snow here was deeper. All the time their eyes were on the steep rocky sides, ever searching for a possible way up.

'I can't go up there! I can't!', Kerry burst out, catching her companion's arm so that he was pulled round to face her. 'Ivan, please try to forgive me. I can hardly walk in this cold, let alone climb!' She searched his face, fearing that anger might make him storm away from her.

'Dear Kerry', he answered gently instead, 'I know only too well how you feel; but it is for Peter – now we have come so far we cannot give up. And there must be a way. There *will* be a way. Just keep on! I feel sure it will not be long now'.

He grasped her hand firmly in his own. How cold it is, she thought to herself; but then she touched her face with her own hand and found it was as if turned to ice. How could she ever hope to find hand-holds on the great smooth wall of stone with hands like these?

They passed under the shadow, the ice thick beneath their feet. Deep white rime sparkled beneath rocks strewn like teeth under the overhanging face; above them, too, on the narrow ledges, a white crust gleamed. The cold now seemed less intense, but the girl still found herself shivering uncontrollably, a gnawing fear in her heart. She plodded on, her breath hissing between her teeth, sliding and falling on the sea of ice; Ivan went before, choosing the way with care. At last he turned and waited for her. There could be no upward path on the first sheer wall they had reached; she placed her numb hands on the rock and felt its terrifying smoothness. Now they turned and made their way along the edge of the south-facing wall, but again every stone seemed locked in place, and the moonlight shone on its polished face. They reached the third wall. All was in blackest shadow as they felt for a way to climb. And then Ivan stumbled on something hard underfoot – a small ledge of rock which gave way even as he touched it. 'The rock is crumbled here!' he exclaimed. 'There may be a path from here – if only I could see!' A moment later he called out excitedly: 'There is a way!'

Kerry saw that he was already higher, that he had found a ledge which held him. And she would have to follow, come what might; there could be no turning back now. She struggled, her nails scratching on the rock, and reached it at last. But now the ledge had become a narrow path; they saw that it had been chipped from the stone, and that it led upwards sharply; they might yet reach the summit safely if they did not miss their way.

For a time it was easy to follow; from the corner of her eye the girl followed Ivan's shadow upwards, step after tiny step, gouging her fingers fiercely into every fissure in the rock above, not once daring to glance down into the gloom and emptiness. All at once she lost her footing and cried out in terror; immediately he was there to hold her fast. Fear took hold of her, and for a moment she stood trembling, unable to move. Gradually the trembling ceased, and she was ready to go on. A wave of gratitude to Ivan for his timely rescue swept over her, and she whispered her thanks.

She dared not think how high they might be now; she would not look below at the void which would swallow her if she should fall. She simply forced herself on and up, on and up; her spirit felt weary beyond anything she had ever known; her feet carried her on as if in a dream.

Then, looking up, she noticed a line of pale gold tingeing the sky, heralding the dawn. Her heart lightened at the sight, for with dawn the chill of night would surely pass, and there would be light to guide them on the final part of the ascent. Slowly the sky brightened, and in a rising wind the last banks of heavy stormclouds rolled away to leave the heavens azure, and the moon fading above the mountains.

Cheered at first, Kerry realised almost at once with a quickly sinking heart that with sunrise Peter might already be dead. She saw that they had not far to go now. Then quite suddenly the climb was over; the last long narrow ledge was past, and then they were over the top and their feet standing gratefully not on stone, but on a broad, flat, grassy meadow. For a moment they threw themselves down, panting, allowing the warm sun to caress their faces. Then they saw ahead a kind of darkness which at once blotted out the relief in their hearts.

Around the four sides of the great carved rock, and embedded in the heart of the stone, there stood a square of rough-hewn pillars, each one standing alone, the first light not yet reaching their ebony core. As they stood up, they saw ahead of them an avenue of higher columns of gleaming ochre, seeming to bend darkly inwards.

In silence and apprehension they began to walk past the first of the giant pillars, standing like impassive guards watching over what looked like gravestones beyond, huge stones that gleamed darkly red in the light. The wind was still; not a breath now stirred on the table-top of the rock; the world seemed asleep. They went on, deeper into the shadow.

'So you dared to come!' A harsh voice startled them, causing them to fall back as a tall, menacing white form advanced from the rocks. A Priest towered above them, his eyes seeming to burn with mocking malevolence. The owl on his shoulder stared at them unblinkingly, the gold of its eyes lit by the fire of the sun. The Priest laughed evilly. They felt infinitely small beside him; his derision reduced them to quaking insignificance. The Priest raised his arm high in the air, and a dozen Priests stepped from the rocks, each with an owl on his shoulder, their eyes and those of the birds gleaming as if with some inner fire of sheer hate. Their mocking laughter turned the very sunlight into darkness.

All at once strength came to Kerry as she thought of Peter.

What did her fear matter, what did anything matter if only he might still be saved? Surely she had nothing to lose; at all costs she must at least make one last attempt, however doomed, to reach the father she loved. Summoning up every last ounce of her courage, she faced the Priests. 'Tell me where Peter is!' she demanded in a strong, clear voice. 'Tell me what you have done with him! You know as well as I do that he doesn't deserve to die!'

The eyes of the Priest towering over her seemed almost to lash her with hatred and fury like the thongs of a whip. He laughed again, his gaze boring into her soul. 'You fool!' he snarled at length. 'Did you really believe you could defy the command of the Voice himself? Can you not feel his power now, weakling, searching you, emptying you of every shred of spirit you ever had? Look at the sky; see that the time of death is already past, that his soul has gone as it was decreed, to the place of service, the Street of Wailing'.

A wave of agony washed over the girl at these words. She fell down in front of the Priest, her head half buried in the grass. Weakness born of hunger and exhaustion threatened to overwhelm her. But the Priest's will commanded her. 'Rise up', he spat at her, 'pass every stone, and you will come to your Peter, and find that my words are the truth'.

'Do not dare to touch her!' Ivan cried out, lunging towards Kerry in a despairing effort to turn her back; but the Priest whirled round upon him so that he now felt the lash of the terrible eyes, and felt his strength ebbing away. Defeated, he was silent and hung his head. Yet in a moment he felt himself forced to look up and meet the gaze he so feared; and it was as if his very heart was being crushed and turned to dust by the venom exuded by a being totally evil.

'I have not sent her to her death', the Priest said then; 'I long to consume you both, worthless ones, by the power that is mine as leader of the Priests – yet I cannot'. Strangely, the last words sounded almost like a plea. Ivan, fearful as he was, found himself nauseated. 'Do you not understand that the Voice must have you first?' the Priest almost wailed. 'Are you so blind that you cannot see how he makes me crave for your blood, yet it is denied me? Surely you must know that it was he who led you here, so that one day he might play with you in his domain?'

The Priest turned abruptly away, and Ivan was free of his eyes, those eyes which had lashed him and all but drained his strength; only the eyes of the owl still devoured him with unblinking malice, as if it too somehow shared in the Voice's dark power. Then suddenly Ivan saw and seized his opportunity. He rushed after Kerry into the avenue of stones, feeling now the eyes burning into his back; and then he was running, running on beyond all the pillars, running oblivious of everything except that he must at all costs reach the girl's side.

She was kneeling on the soft grass in silence, heedless of his presence, the Priests standing behind her and the stone of sacrifice before her, crimson with the blood of her people, the Unborn. For a moment he could not bring himself to look upon the face of Peter, could not endure to see closed in death the gentle eyes which had in turn sparkled with joy or wept in sadness in accord with the people he loved. At last he had to look; and he saw the cold, pale face, and the frozen line of blood which ran round the neck. Feelings of anger and helplessness welled up in him; could deeds so evil ever be forgotten?

But Kerry did not seem either to hear or to see; her hands, frozen to a strange blue-whiteness, reached out and met the old hands which once had comforted and soothed her, which had both welcomed and at times scolded her. The boy was frightened by her aspect; her face was as ashen as her hands. It was as if every drop of blood had been drained from her body and she had been left, preserved, like some pathetic being trapped between the tide of life and death. Tears were frozen on her cheeks, yet she wept no longer; and she seemed to gaze beyond Peter's body, beyond the last green of the mountain table-top, seeing perhaps some invisible image that still lived and spoke. The wind, a light breeze which had begun to blow, lifted her soft hair; and it seemed to sigh as if in mourning for Peter.

Ivan rose at last from his knees, gently raised the girl and helped her to stand beside him, facing the long, eerie avenue of stones which appeared at times almost to bow to one another. Past the leering faces of the Priests he led her silently, past the

eyes that gleamed evilly and darkly as if they would reach out
to scorch their very souls. And finally they came to the Priest
who had first mocked them, and Ivan again met the flaming
violence of his burning look, and summoned all his courage to
battle against the power wielded to subdue his spirit.

'Tell your foul master we are coming!' he cried with all his
might. 'Tell him there has been enough murder, enough break-
ing of hearts, enough death! Let him know that my people, the
Unborn, are crying out for freedom, and will not be denied. He
may take my life if he wishes; I am willing to give it up for the
sake of the Unborn, that this land may one day be theirs. Peter
did not deserve to die – but he did not die in vain! Remember
that, remember it!' Ivan wrenched himself away, still leading
Kerry by the hand.

'Wait!' cried the Priest, and the word was like ice, and they
stopped and waited by the edge of the table-top. 'I will tell him
what you said, and he will laugh, and wait for you with
pleasure in the Underland. The Unborn are his, fool! And he
will not give them up for the offered life of any being. You
waste your weak breath; you have not the power to open the
door of his dwelling. His might would shatter you into a million
million fragments of dust! Remember this – it is not your will
that draws you to him; it is his own leading and deception that
make you seek out the way to his throne, for it is he who
desires to see you and test your love for your people – *his*
people! And when he is done with you, weakling, I will feast
on your soul!'

He did not say any more, nor did he try to stop them; nor
did Ivan turn again. He moved away and Kerry, still half-dazed,
followed him. Together they left the high rock plateau and came
again to the steep ledges that would lead to the plains far below.
Ivan went first, forcing his fingers into the fissures in the rocks,
mindful always of her safety as well as his own; and she came
slowly after, weeping bitterly.

Chapter 6

The Snows

It was worse to descend that smooth wall in the light of the new day. Memories of Peter haunted them; the emptiness of the ledges they still had to tread was apparent as it had not been on the ascent. Ivan was fearful for his companion; she seemed no more than half awake, scarcely alert to the danger, almost certainly at times blinded by tears. Yet they must go on; to delay would be dangerous, and far away in the western reaches of the sky the first angry clouds of another storm could all too clearly be seen. He knew well that the girl could not endure such a storm as had assailed them the night before; indeed he too felt utterly weak with exhaustion, battered after the confrontation with the Priests, and doubtful of his own endurance. At least they were still alive; and he closed his mind to his weariness and pressed on slowly and carefully.

Somehow they reached the base of the mountain in safety, Kerry half-stumbling down the last treacherous ledges of rock. Wearily but with a sense of great relief, they turned westwards, trudging in silence over the snow-swept plain, heads bowed, their resolve at times dangerously near to snapping until with an effort they remembered the reason for their journey. And when at last they looked back, the stone walls, bright in the golden light of the sun, looked as ever unscalable, and the memory of the mountain's grassy rooftop meadow like something they had dreamed.

They came at length to the frozen reaches of the Arxia, twin of the Poleria that came gushing in spring from the Shallowlands, becoming no longer the Quenil or the white-flecked Tremos, but its own river. It was dead now, locked in ice; and yet the days were coming when in the north the first snows would melt, and the cold grey waters would come tumbling again from the ice-bound hills. Now the sun shone on its smooth reaches, the wide sheets of ice made whiter by the recent snows, and all was utterly quiet; but thick storm-clouds were rolling nearer, with the dire warning of what was to come. Faintly, almost inaudibly, as they reached the banks, the sound of a trickle of water could be heard under the ice.

Kerry was now walking ahead of Ivan, walking as if she neither knew nor cared where she was going. He had noted her sunken eyes, reflecting the anguish she was feeling; but they had not talked again about Peter, and he followed her in silence, not wishing to intrude on her thoughts. She did not even pause as they reached the river bank and she stepped down; she neither slowed nor quickened her pace, but began to walk across the gleaming slabs of ice as if she still had snow beneath her feet. Ivan came behind her, his cloak wrapped tightly about him against the bitter chill, his eyes searching the ice, wary of any flaw. All at once he heard a noise ahead, a noise so slight that he did not pause, nor even look up, nor think of it as a warning. In a moment, the girl was swallowed up by the Arxia. The ice had given way under her weight, and she had fallen, gasping, into the freezing water. She called out in terror, but her cry was lost as her head vanished beneath the ice. At once the boy lay flat and flung his arms deep into the water, desperate to hold her; he caught her hand and grasped it, and with every ounce of strength he could muster, raised her from the river and on to the firm ice. She was weeping with no sound at all.

They reached the far bank at last, the first angry flakes of snow falling about them from the wall of increasing blackness above. Ivan forgot the snow, forgot everything except the girl who lay shivering in his arms, cold as death. 'Kerry, Kerry, forgive me!', he whispered. 'I should have led the way; I should have seen the danger in time and warned you. I have driven you too hard – so hard that you could not see it for yourself. Oh Kerry, forgive me!' But her eyes were shut and she seemed to have slipped away from him.

He went on shaking her and rubbing her numbed hands, fearing that she would die if he did not force her to keep on fighting against the intense cold. Her eyelids flickered open at last, but her eyes were blank, her face almost the colour of the ice. For a moment she smiled weakly as if recognising the trouble in his face; then she seemed to look through and beyond him, perhaps to some unseen land of warmth and light, far from the cruelty of winter storms. After this, nothing he did would waken her again. She seemed lost to him. The wind, too, was rising, sweeping down from the frozen north and howling eerily across the flat wastes.

Bracing himself, he picked Kerry's inert form up in his arms and began to plod through the snow. The wall of blackness now made it seem as if night had returned already. On and on he battled; although the girl was light, his arms soon began to feel heavy as lead, and he was gasping, feeling with each laboured breath that his strength could not last much longer. All the time the fury of the storm was increasing, the wind becoming ever more powerful.

At last he found himself in an area of massive rocks which loomed up suddenly, seemingly all around him. His tired heart leapt – surely there was just a chance that shelter could be found, a respite from the snow and violent wind? Behind a huge rock, in a fissure where the storm could not reach her, he laid Kerry down with infinite gentleness, and went to search for a refuge. To his great relief, he found one almost at once – a small but high-roofed cave with a dry floor; the entrance, though, was far too wide, and he at once set to work to build a wall of frozen snow and ice, tearing with his hands until it was high enough to complete the cave, leaving only a narrow aperture. He did not notice that his hands were bleeding, in his relief that there would now be a safe place in which they could rest. He quickly returned to the girl, picked her up again and laid her gently on the cave's floor. For a time he was content to lie beside her, savouring the solace of the shelter and peace.

He watched her face, allowing his thoughts to drift as he re-lived the agony of her cry, and the way she had looked pitifully up at him when the freezing water had taken her. He realised with deep remorse that the fault was his, that he had been too imprisoned within his own thoughts to warn her, or to go ahead that she might be safe. She now seemed as far away as ever and did not move. And yet as he looked down on her he felt that he had never seen her so much at peace; and it was he who felt the bitter loneliness of the silence, the great need of comfort, the longing for his own peace. The desire to rest was strong; it would have been so easy to lie back and listen to the winds raging over the plains as he shut his eyes to sleep – to sleep perhaps for ever.

Determinedly he roused himself and set about searching the cavern for anything that could be burned, for he knew Kerry's desperate need of warmth. Fortunately there were plenty of small dry sticks at the back of the cave, as well as some brushwood, but he must leave her again to go and search for some more substantial wood. He faced the howling blast again. Once more, to his relief, he found what he sought almost at once – the stump of a dead tree that was rotten and crumbling with age. He lost no time in dragging it into their shelter; if only he could get a fire going with the dry twigs, this could be expected to burn for many hours. First he carefully removed the girl's sodden cloak and hung it up in the cave; then he gently wrapped his own cloak around her. Next he set about making fire from the sticks. Thankfully he found he had not lost his old skill, won so dearly during the hard years in the caves; soon a red glow began to curl about the waiting wood. Shivering now, he set brushwood and more twigs carefully around the flame. And as the first smoke began to drift upwards, he was at last able to lie back in peace and close his eyes, re-living the memory of that endless day. He would sleep in blissful comfort while the storm raged outside. He gently reached over and pulled a fold of his cloak over him, sharing it with Kerry that he might ease the chill he himself felt and would know if she were to waken and need him.

And so he slept; and beyond the walls of the shelter the storm eased at length; the wind dropped and the snow ceased, to give way to a clear sky and the moon coming up over the silver line of the distant hills. He slept long, then half-awoke to rekindle the dying fire, and slept again. This time he awoke with his tiredness gone. He could scarcely believe that there could be such utter quietness after the endless torment of the wind. He arose noiselessly, almost afraid to break the silence, his feet whispering in the snow as he stepped outside. So clear was the light that he could see the further peaks in every direction; each summit was etched perfectly against the sky. He stood, shivering, up to his ankles in the snow, looking upwards, awed by the silence and the beauty of the heavens. All the weariness of soul which had so oppressed him on the previous day seemed to ebb away. This was what he had come to find; this was the loveliness known till now only in dreams; this was the reason he had braved the power of the Voice and fought to leave the despair of the caves! This was the land in which the Unborn should live.

His feet slipped easily through the snow. Not a sound could be heard. He went on for a time, heedless of the cold, exulting in all he saw around him, until he came to a stream, its waters choked by snow and ice. As he watched, a creature appeared on the bank, ploughing and struggling through the high-piled snow, to dive at last into an ice-free pool. He saw that it was an otter. In delight he watched the lithe form playing in the pool; he held his breath lest his intrusion might frighten it away, but with a thrill of joy saw the silver-dappled head rise again from the water. Time seemed to stand still.

Ivan was oblivious of all the world in those enchanted moments, having eyes only for the grace and agility of the beautiful creature as it revelled in the rippled waters of the pool, turning and twisting and diving with perfect ease. Unable to help himself, he started towards the stream. For a moment it seemed as if the whole world was still, as man met beast and looked into each other's eyes; the planed head looked erect from the water and the eyes, more puzzled perhaps than fearful, seemed to search the stranger's, unblinking. He marvelled at the trusting innocence of its gaze; yet almost immediately it was gone, and it appeared to Ivan that a bond had snapped and that he was somehow the poorer for its going.

He felt forlorn as he turned away, and was again conscious of the biting cold. At once the thought of Kerry returned to him. What was he to do? The burden of her plight lay heavily on him; he blamed himself bitterly for her state, and knew that he must at all costs find help for her, even if he should perish in the attempt. But which way should he take? He felt that he already knew the way, and, recalling the words of the Priest, 'surely you must know that it was the Voice who led you here', he shuddered. Was it true? Were they really being led, inexorably, to the domain of the evil ruler of the land? And yet, if they were not, how could they hope to defy and overthrow him? He must go on; and since Kerry could not walk, he must carry her.

Slowly he returned to the cave. He bent over the girl, who had not moved at all, and as he saw her face, pale as death, it seemed to him that he no longer heard her breath; frenziedly he began to shake her, calling her name in a desperate effort to reach through to her. For an instant the pale eyelids flickered and she spoke faintly as if from a far place, 'The Voice, oh Ivan, I cannot escape from the Voice . . .' Then she had again slipped far away. Kneeling beside her, he tried to make her drink the last of the water in the skin he had brought; seeing it was useless to offer her even a morsel of food, he opened the satchel and ate a piece of bread himself. Then gently, wrapping her now-dry cloak around her, he lifted her like a little child in his arms, held her close and bore her tenderly out of the cave which had sheltered them.

To his dismay he found that the storm was rising again. He knew there was little hope of making progress if the wind should reach the violence of the previous day, yet if he lingered here another day, help might come too late for the girl. He began to walk across the frozen plain, trying to steady his mind with childhood memories of Kerry. He was half dreaming, his weary mind momentarily soothed, when a new sound came to him above the shrieking blasts, a noise as of howling voices above the wind, and at one with their chaos. As he stopped, fear gripped his throat; he heard at first only his own gasping, tortured breath; then the sound came again. Almost before his tired brain had taken in the danger, the wolves were upon him, their snarling fangs leering, their howls urgent now with the lust for blood.

Hardly knowing what he did, Ivan set Kerry down gently and reached for his knife, his only weapon. In that very instant he was fighting for his life as a great wolf leaped at him, toppling him and almost crushing him with its weight. Then all was confusion; afterwards he could recall little except a terrifying struggle, and a moment of pure agony as the beast clawed his wrist. And then it seemed as if supernatural strength came to him, as he jabbed the knife with all his might into the brute's throat. Blood spurted everywhere; with a great howl the wolf rolled over, dead. Still dazed, Ivan found himself sobbing as he drew out the knife; and as he rose at last, he scarcely took in that the other wolves had slunk silently away, and that Kerry still lay nearby with a peaceful smile on her lips.

His one thought then was to find water – not so much to wash his bleeding hand as in a desperate urge to wipe out the memory of his violent deed; he wept again as he remembered the look which had so recently passed between him and the silvery otter, seeming to vow a new bond between animal and man, and an end to all killing. He washed away the blood in a kind of ritual of repentance, then slowly made his way back to Kerry and lay down for a few moments of rest. Summoning all his strength and striving to forget his deathly weariness, he picked Kerry up and began to walk through the snow, determined to think of nothing at all except the need to keep going. The wind seemed to mock him, driving down from the hills and tormenting him, buffeting him ceaselessly, giving him no peace. He bent his head and battled on. His arms ached; at first he resolved not to give in to this weakness, but there came a time when he was forced to lay Kerry down while he rested. Then he was on his way again, stumbling onwards for what seemed like an eternity, hour after hour after hour, past hunger, past fear, past thought. Whenever the ache in his arms became intolerable, he would lay her down for a few moments; then he would battle onwards again. At last he lost all sense of time, even forgot where he was or why he must keep on.

It seemed a long time later that he became dimly aware that something was different. He began to realise that the wind had dropped; the needles of ice no longer tormented him. Then, hardly able to believe it, he saw before him trees, and through their boughs, the last dying ochres and crimsons of the sun as it sank beneath the western mountains. He had been walking all day. He came to the shadows of the great still pines like a victor, passing beneath their needled branches that were heavy with the weight of gathered snow; blissfully he reached the safety and silence of what seemed to him like another world. He felt at one with the silent trees which appeared like sentinels, standing against the hostile might of winter. Beauty lay hidden in the last rays of the sun, in the gnarled boughs, in the pools and cataracts of a stream that danced on its way swollen with the first melting snow. Somehow it seemed that the full malice of winter had not reached the soul of this forest; was it too much to hope that the Voice had no power over this place of peace, that his darkness had not fallen upon it? Hope began to stir in his weary heart.

At first he did not perceive the fragrance of the forest; he walked on, enjoying the feel of the carpet of needles under his tired feet; but then he became aware of it and stopped, and lifted his head, like a stag hearing a sound from afar. Once again he laid Kerry down while for a few moments he rested, drinking in the sight and sound and scent of the pines, which seemed like balm to his tired spirit. Then, refreshed, he picked her up and continued on his way.

A few moments later he heard rustlings in the glades, restless patterings which puzzled him at first; then all at once the clearing he entered was encircled by the gentle muzzles of deer. To his surprise they did not run away as he approached, but came towards him almost as if they knew and welcomed him. He did not understand how this could be, yet he felt his heart lift with joy; laying Kerry down on a soft bed of moss, he went closer and touched the soft fur on their brows, while they pressed closely around him as if in welcome. A feeling of great peace washed over him and he would gladly have lingered in their midst, but, mindful of the girl's need, he picked her up and continued on his way through the forest. Looking round, he saw that they were following.

Night came, and the moon shone through the canopy of the trees, bathing the animals in its silver light. The forest was now so still that when he stopped and the gentle animals once again encircled him, he could hear their soft breathing. He had not known there could be such harmony between man and beast;

again he felt a sense of joy and peace which brought refreshment and eased his tiredness.

As night deepened and a thousand stars glittered in the sky, a tall figure came swiftly through the trees towards him. He began to run as he approached, then, as he came near, to the boy's amazement he bowed low. His face was radiant as he raised his head again and looked intently into Ivan's face, and then allowed his gaze to travel round the circle of deer surrounding him.

'Welcome, Fawnleader!' he cried then in a clear and joyous voice. 'Winter's power will be broken now that you have come! Spring is at hand, when our land will come to full life again! I greet you in the name of the Pyrians, the last of the people of this ancient land to stand against the evil of the Voice'.

Ivan, uncomprehending but with a profound feeling of relief such as he had never before experienced, could say nothing.

But as the tall old man turned and led the way onwards, he put his weariness behind him and followed; and the deer gathered round him and followed too.

As the strange procession advanced, the boy's thoughts were in turmoil. He was too tired to grapple with the mystery, but in bewilderment he kept returning to the old man's words. 'Fawnleader' – what could this mean? He saw that the deer had no fear of him; they pressed close to him, and it had been almost as if they recognised him as a friend. But what had he to do with winter, or the coming of spring? Wearily he gave up trying to understand and stumbled on.

The trees opened at length into a wide clearing, in the midst of which a great fire burned. Round it he saw a circle of white-clad men and women who awaited their coming in silence. As Ivan approached, faintness threatened to overcome him; the flames seemed to twist and turn like his fevered thoughts, and the white figures to swim in a sea of fire. He staggered and stood still while the leader spoke again in his clear, ringing voice. 'No words are sufficient to tell what your coming means to my people, Fawnleader', he said. There was a chorus of assent from the circle of his people. 'The signs of old are true', he continued. Again a wave of faintness passed over Ivan. Swaying now, he held Kerry close for a moment and then, as blackness began to close in on him, he managed to whisper: 'Take her, please look after her'. At once a man stepped forward and lifted the girl from his arms. Then the tall leader caught him as he fell.

Chapter 7

Celroc

The morning was already well advanced when Ivan awoke. He lay at first half-awake, savouring a feeling of well-being and peace which was altogether new to him. How quiet it was! The graceful forms of deer had filled his dreams; he could see them still, with their fawns at their feet, as they had followed him over what had seemed like endless plains of snow and ice. Half-dreaming still, he began to see in memory a fire burning, with a circle of people round it; had that too been a dream? And a tall figure in a shining white cloak which billowed about him as he walked. Then he became aware of a kind of fragrance all around him, a scent compounded of resin and fresh-cut pine wood, and moss, with its clean freshness; he felt the softness underneath him, and found that he was lying on a bed of moss. Had he fallen asleep in the forest? Suddenly he was fully awake. Kerry! Where was she? Now he remembered! He had let her fall from his arms! He jumped up, conscious at once of the ache still left after carrying her. Then he saw her.

She was lying nearby, on a bed of moss, with a wrap of fur covering her. He went and bent down like a child beside her. 'Oh Kerry, Kerry', he whispered, kneeling and caressing her brow with his hands. He felt a wave of pure love for her sweep over him. Had he then borne her through the winter storms in vain? So still she lay, seeming so distant in unconsciousness; he hardly saw her breathe, scarcely felt the faint flutter of her pulse that still beat like the wings of a wounded bird.

A slight sound behind made him look up. It was the old man, standing in the doorway of the rough wooden hut in which they had spent the night. 'We have brought you some food, my son', he said in his resonant voice. A young boy entered, bearing a wooden bowl of milk, some bread and several small eggs. Ivan suddenly realised how hungry he was – how long since he had last eaten! He began to thank his host, but was quickly interrupted.

'I beg your forgiveness', the leader began. 'When you came through the trees with the deer all around you, I was filled with such joy that all courtesy departed from me: instead of relieving you of your burden, realising how near exhaustion you must be, I turned and ran to tell my people the good news! I should have seen your plight and taken the girl from you . . . what is her name?' he added.

'She is called Kerry', answered the boy, 'and I am Ivan'.

'You shall be Ivan no longer, my son,' said the man with a radiant smile, 'for you are our long-awaited Fawnleader!'

'Please,' begged Ivan, 'I remember that you called me by that name when we met. Will you now explain, for I do not understand at all?'

'While you eat I shall tell you,' he replied. Ivan wasted no time in beginning his delicious meal, while the old man began his tale.

'My name is Falliope', he explained. 'We are the last people of this land of Pyrus not to fall under the will of the evil Voice; yet our time is short, like the last leaves that remain before the coming of the winter winds. Still, we have reason to stand firm in our faith, as did our fathers and the men who led our proud people in days long since forgotten, when trees covered the wide plains and the fawns walked safe beneath their branches. In those days there lived a man called Celroc, and his words spoke courage to the people of old, for he was a great prophet. He said that a time would come in the midst of winter when a young man, a stranger, would come through the trees carrying in his arms a woman deep in sickness, and at his back the fawns of the forest walking freely. All down the years, my son, my people have looked for the fulfilment of this prophecy, for it is of great importance – you see, there is much more: he foretold that this young man, whom he called the Fawnleader, would be the one to save the people of Pyrus from the evil power of the Voice!'

Ivan listened fascinated; he watched the old man's face,

amazed to see that his eyes sparkled like those of a youth. 'But how?' he enquired, 'how was this young man to deliver the people from their bondage? Was he to have some special powers?'

'Indeed he would be given special powers', was the reply. 'It was prophesied that he would be able to blow this ancient horn wrought by the people of old – no man has ever blown it – and at this signal a beautiful white deer, called the White Fawn, which it is said first roamed the woods and glades of Pyrus, would come!'

'And what then?' asked the boy, now feeling himself caught up in the excitement. 'What part was to be played by this deer?'

'It was said that the Fawn alone knew the hiding-place of a beautiful dark jewel. And it would lead the young man to that place, and the jewel would be the means of destroying the might of the Voice!' the old man concluded triumphantly.

There was silence for a time while Ivan, awed, attempted to digest the full import of what he had heard. Falliope and his people actually believed he might be the Fawnleader! The idea both excited and frightened him. Aloud he said: 'But what if you are mistaken, and I am not the one you have waited for?'

The old man shook his head; his eyes still sparkled with joy. 'Ah, but the signs of old are true', he declared. 'In you, all has surely been fulfilled! Never have the fawns of the forest welcomed anyone as they have you! So you can see,' he finished breathlessly, 'why my old heart leapt with joy when I saw you come, and I all but ran to tell my people that the Fawnleader so long awaited was here, and why I failed to show you the courtesy you deserved'.

Ivan was speechless. Again he sat lost in thought, trying to take in the strange words, at one moment afraid and at the next feeling his heart lift with hope. Then Falliope was holding out the ancient horn in his hand. To gain time, the boy examined the ornate workmanship, turning it round and round, and finally saying diffidently: 'I have never blown a horn in my life, Falliope.'

'Take it and blow with all your strength, Fawnleader!' cried the irrepressible old man, 'and you will earn forever the gratitude of the people of Pyrus!'

Still Ivan sat unmoving. 'And if I am not the one?' he said again.

'Then the Fawn will not come – but I for one do not doubt that it will, and the dark gem will be found. Ah, how I have longed for that day!'

Ivan was not yet ready. He crossed to Kerry's side, and bent over her still form. The thought had come to him that if all this really were true, he was being asked to leave her, for how long he had no idea. Was she not more precious than anything else? What if she should awaken and find him gone?

'If, as you say, the White Fawn comes, we must follow', he said slowly. 'That will mean leaving Kerry. How can I do that when, as you see, she is ill and in great need?'

Falliope showed no hesitation. 'Our people have great skill with plants', he replied. 'She has already been given a healing draught, and she will recover; but she needs to be nursed with great care, and I promise you that the women of Pyrus will look after her well'. Falliope finished speaking and turned a look of such pleading on Ivan that he could not bear to keep him waiting a moment longer. He took the horn and blew with all his might.

As he blew, a strange sensation of having been given new powers came to him: it was as if he could, for these moments, see the whole land of Pyrus as it responded to the long-awaited note. Like the opening of great gates that held back the flow of a stream, the music of the horn resounded in the valleys, and echoed from the heights of the mountains. It seemed as if the whole world heard that sound. The deer that drank from the ice-thick pools lifted their heads, turning as if roused by a summons; the tall pines awoke from the sleep of long years as if hearing the call of spring. Ivan could not any longer doubt that the words of Celroc were indeed being fulfilled. He shrank from the task ahead and yet awaited it eagerly.

And on the slopes of a rugged hillside whose trees were bowed beneath their load of snow, a white beast lifted its head at the sound of the horn and came swiftly over the plains, bounding over the icy streams. Still Ivan blew, and still the land waited, held under the enchantment of that summons. Then at last there was silence, and he handed back the horn to the old man. Suddenly a silvery white beast stood in the shadow of the pines, and as Falliope turned and saw that it was indeed the White Fawn, he laughed outright like a child, to see the fulfilment of that for which he had longed all his life.

'Come, Fawnleader', he cried joyfully, 'now there can be no more doubt in your heart that you are he. Let us leave now, you and I together, on the journey ordained for you – see, the White Fawn is waiting to lead the way! Cyra', he said to the youth who had brought the food, 'bring provisions for us; and tell our people to come and wish our Fawnleader well!'

Almost at once it seemed that the glade had filled with men, women and children who stretched out hands in greeting to Ivan, and whose faces showed that they shared their leader's joyful eagerness. Then a satchel of food was handed to him, and without a moment's delay they set off, a chorus of farewells following them, Falliope leading the way with the strong tread of a young man.

At first they walked in silence, savouring the beauty of the morning. Ivan was conscious of a new strength within himself; he marvelled that the exhaustion of the previous day had so soon left him; even his arms, aching because of carrying Kerry, were now completely restored. More than this, the sense he had had while he blew the ancient horn of the whole land of Pyrus re-awakening from the grip of winter was still strongly with him. They neared a river, and saw the White Fawn standing by its banks, almost silver in the bright light: for a moment it stood, silhouetted; then it bent to the water and drank. With a single leap it was away, bounding across the icy pools and into the forest again. As they reached the river, the boy heard its tumbling water and was conscious that it held a note of joyous release; it seemed to sing as it danced along. It seemed too as if spring itself sighed through the branches of the pines, while snow fell in heavy piles from the trees to become water again and run chuckling in streamlets; and in the bright daylight the trees had a new glory, their branches taking on a sheen of pure gold.

As they strode on in the path of the beast, Ivan saw that Falliope was deep in his own thoughts; he appeared to have no need of speech, but his face still held a look of radiant hope.

The boy allowed his own thoughts to return to Kerry – refreshed
and invigorated as he was, a shadow crossed his heart at the
memory of her. Was it possible that she would, as Falliope
believed, come back to health again? And were the Pyrians
really skilled physicians? As he had knelt to bid her goodbye,
he had touched her brow and found it hot – was she perhaps
beginning a fever, and would she call out for him and know
him gone?

The troubled reverie was interrupted by the old man, who
seemed to have become aware of his presence again. He pointed
to the noble animal running lightly through the trees, keeping
always well ahead of them. 'See, my son', he said, 'the Fawn
leads us to the North'. After another silence he continued:
'Forgive me that in my eagerness to hurry you on your journey
I have not yet learned anything of you and your companion.
You fulfilled the ancient prophecy of Celroc; you came to us
through the forest, bearing in your arms the maiden he himself
saw in dreams. Yet beyond that I know nothing. That you are
not of our people I know from your manner and your garb.
Where then did you come from, at a time when our winter
storms on the plains must have been at their most cruel?'

Briefly Ivan hesitated before replying. He recalled the emptiness and hopelessness and darkness in which their childhood
had been passed, the agony suffered by Maria, the anguish of
the loss of Peter. How could this old man possibly understand?
How could he ever know the suffering of those children who
were denied the world of life, condemned to exist without the
sight of the sun, moon and stars? At last he answered, and
there was neither anger nor bitterness in his voice.

'Kerry and I are of the children of the Unborn, outcasts from
another world, prisoners of the Voice. The Priests rule over all
our people, forcing us to live under the mountains in fear so
that we may never escape to live in the true land, this land of
beauty. Every month they come to one of the villages in the
caves and take away one person to be killed when the moon is
full. I believe it might have gone on in this way for ever, with
the Priests slowly killing our people, and our villagers in their
hunger and despair sometimes fighting one another, even killing one another, as they struggle for food. Peter was the leader

in our village, and it was he alone who kept us together, forbidding us to submit our wills to the Voice who would have driven us to madness by his whispering in our ears, whisperings which were always of doom and destruction. And most of all Peter was a father to Kerry, always loving her and teaching her to care for others. Then one terrible day the Priests came and took him as their victim. We could bear it no longer! We left, after a struggle against the Voice who would have stopped our escape from the caves. We wanted somehow to find the Voice and offer ourselves for the lives of the Unborn; but first we wanted desperately to save Peter'. Ivan stopped.

'And did you find him?' asked Falliope eagerly. Sadly, Ivan shook his head.

'We were too late; he had been killed on the rock of sacrifice by the Priests. But they did not harm us, and so we came on through cruel storms and endless snow and ice. Then, when our strength was almost gone, Kerry fell through the ice into the freezing river, and I was not able to revive her. So I carried her. The rest you know, Falliope – how glad I was to find you and your people to care for us in our great need'.

'My people and yours share much', answered the old man in a voice of compassion and understanding. 'Yours are helpless against the power of the Voice, condemned to live under the constant threat of the Priests; and my own, because we must move deeper into the woods with every year that passes, further into sanctuary that his shadow may not fall on us also. Now we are the last free people of the land. Word came to us from the people of Pyrus, the sacred city of the ancient race who roamed the wide, empty Strells of the South to the Northern Crests – and terrible news it was. The Priests had come by night to the valley, the Priests with their staffs and the white owls on their shoulders; and they brought fire and burned the city, leaving it ruined and lost. You see, Fawnleader, once our own people lived in Pyrus, the ancient city, until the day when Celroc led them to the edge of the Woods of Fall; and since then they have waited for the day when his horn would sound again. Our hearts were burdened by the knowledge that the evil ones would seek us out also, that one day we would be driven away from our homes, the pines would be laid waste and the fawns scattered. But now, since you have come, we have hope again!'

All day long they followed the White Fawn, stopping only to rest briefly, eat some food and drink from a stream; always the White Fawn would be seen ahead, sometimes in a clearing in the forest, at other times standing on rising ground, erect, its silvery head turned to the North. Now they were becoming tired. The old man's step had lost its earlier spring; Ivan too had begun to tire, and with the approach of darkness they had begun to think longingly of rest. They came to a rocky ridge and saw below them on the open plains a wide lake above which flocks of birds soared. Their hearts leapt as they looked to the North far beyond and saw a magnificent mountain which seemed to rise to the skies.

'Ah, my friend,' cried the old man with a note almost of reverence in his voice, 'there before us is the mountain of the eagles, Mount Gilrene! Surely the White Fawn leads us there – perhaps indeed beyond – to take you to find the precious stone which holds the key to freedom for us all!'

'I should like to know much more of this stone you speak of, Falliope', said Ivan.

'We know only what was said by Celroc', answered the old man. 'There is a jewel which will be given into the care of our Fawnleader, and no-one else; with it he will be able to destroy the power of the Voice. No more is known, although our people have their own beliefs about it; but we have always held that it would be the White Fawn who would lead the way to where it rests'.

Now they had left the pines far behind, and were traversing the plains. The Fawn had gone ahead of them like a silver arrow, making straight for the mountain. The lake shimmered, far across the wastes; all else seemed empty; nothing met the eye until it rested on the faint outline of an awe-inspiring range – the sharp peaks and spines of the Northern Ice-Crests. Ivan shivered, recalling with horror the climb with Kerry to the rock of sacrifice: if the White Fawn should indeed lead them to Mount Gilrene, he dared not think what terrors such an ascent might bring.

All the time he was aware that with darkness falling they

would soon have to find a place to rest. Ivan wondered whether the White Fawn, now running so gracefully before them as if impatient to fulfil its destiny, would wait for them if they slept for several hours. His thoughts were interrupted by the old man, who had stopped and was gazing, rapt, at the stars. 'See, my friend,' he said softly, 'far in the North you can make out the three stars of the Warriors – Ammon, Mistrin, and Ceregon. And there, as my father often told me when I was a child, above the highest point of Mount Gilrene, is Dreambringer, the brightest star of the heavens, which burns like a gem. Are they not beautiful?' Together they sat for a time lost in the beauty of the night sky.

Silently then, for both were weary, they went on towards the lake. To Ivan it seemed like many hours before they reached its shores. The plains around it were bare except for a single clump of trees close to the water; there they would make their bed. Ivan gathered some dry rushes from the lakeside to form a rough couch on which the old man lay down gratefully. They ate their meagre supper with few words spoken. Soon, wrapped in their cloaks, both were fast asleep. Ivan dreamed vividly of Kerry; she was strong and well, laughing, running through the pines, chasing a graceful animal – a white deer whose coat shone like silver.

Chapter 8

Mount Gilrene

Ivan awoke to find the sun shining on his face; the sensation was so new and so delightful that for a few moments he lay still, enjoying it to the full, and looking lazily at the blue waters of the lake with the birds wheeling gracefully overhead. Then he saw that Falliope was awake, staring intently in the direction of Mount Gilrene. Turning to the boy, he said: 'See, Fawnleader, the White Fawn awaits us!' Ivan, amazed at the range of the old man's vision, soon picked out the tiny white spot which was the deer; he laughed at himself for imagining for a moment that it pawed the ground in impatience for them to follow. The thought was still enough to dispel his ease; feelings of apprehension at what might lie ahead were mixed with eagerness to be off on their mission. Soon they had eaten some bread and drunk from the lake, and they were on their way, making for the awe-inspiring mountain with its huge boulders and frowning walls.

Almost at once the old man began to speak. 'My son', he said quietly, 'I have two things of great importance to say to you. As you can see, I am no longer young; yet when you came to us in the forest and later, when you blew the horn of Celroc, I was filled with great joy, and a new strength came to me. It was as if my youth returned. Alas, it was not so for long! By the time we reached our resting-place last night, I was again an old man. Today I am once more refreshed. But as you can see, we still have a goodly way to go before we reach even the first slopes of Mount Gilrene – and that is where I feel sure the White Fawn is leading us. Indeed, it could even be further – to the great Ice Crests which you see beyond. What I say to you is this – do not be concerned for me at all. I now feel certain that at some point in our journey my strength will fail; then you must leave me and go on – the quest is yours alone. You are our Fawnleader, and must fulfil your destiny!' Ivan hesitated before replying. He knew that what Falliope said might well be true; yet his heart quailed at the thought of going alone into the unknown. And the old man – how would he fare if he were left weary and spent on a mountain such as this?

'Let us hope you are mistaken, Falliope,' he said at last. 'You must know how grateful I am that you are with me; it distresses me even to think of our parting.'

'Still, my son,' persisted the old man, 'I wish you to promise that you will leave me if it should be necessary.' Ivan promised with reluctance. 'There is something else I feel you must know,' continued Falliope. 'As you see, the sun shines now and all looks fair; yet I do not believe this calmness will last. You must be warned, my friend. You face the Voice, a truly terrible foe. It is to bring about his downfall that the jewel is hidden, awaiting your coming. Mark my words well, Fawnleader; he will not easily allow it to fall into your hands! I fear a storm.'

Ivan, looking all around at the beauty and peace, was almost tempted to laugh; but a shadow crossed his heart again at the mention of the Voice – could he ever forget the vile being whose whispers had so marred their young lives in the caves? A mighty foe indeed! But what choice was there except to go on? Briefly he remembered the words of Maria, and strong resolution returned: for all of the Unborn, he must not fail, even if it cost his life. He did not answer Falliope, and they went on over meadows of wind-lifted flowers and grasses, the silent lake now well below them like a mirror in the sun. High above, among the first rocks at the base of the mountain, they could clearly see the White Fawn moving with ease and grace.

No more words passed between them as they climbed towards the rocks. Ivan thought of Kerry as he had last seen her, so far away in unconsciousness, endearing in her helplessness: would he ever see her again? He could not imagine life without her, his dear companion of childhood, sharer of all the pain of life in the darkness. To his own surprise he felt a lifting of the heart as assurance seemed to come that she would indeed recover; he could not tell why he felt thus. Falliope's gentle people would look after her well. His reverie was interrupted by a sudden realisation that the sky was becoming overcast, and a wind was beginning to blow. He looked sharply at Falliope, but the old man said nothing. By the time they had reached the rocks, the sun had been swallowed in a huge phalanx of cloud that lay black in the west, and the peak, hard and pitiless, seemed to rise up endlessly before them.

The great rocks which stood on the ledges high above now looked to Ivan like skulls; he could not suppress a shudder. Now there was no grass beneath their feet, no pine needles to cushion them as in the forest, only unending slopes of scree, stretching higher and higher above them. Finally the sun was altogether gone, and with a rising wind there came squalls of freezing hail which all but blinded them as they laboured upwards. Ivan looked anxiously at his companion; he was breathing fast, but as yet showed no signs of distress. Then the wind and hail eased, and they caught a glimpse of silvery white outlined for an instant on the shoulder of the mountain; then like an arrow, the deer was gone from sight as it bounded towards the snow-filled gullies.

There for a long time they rested and shared their food, and drank gratefully from a rushing stream. Ivan was watching the old man closely; he still looked well, and his eyes were bright. So they went on, higher and higher, the wind still strong but the hail now abated so that their vision was clear. The lake was far below them now, a tiny speck of darkness. Then came the chill of dusk and the rising rasp of the wind. Ivan caught sight of a hawk silhouetted above the high ridge of the mountain; silently he pointed it out to Falliope. It circled like a pale ghost in the emptiness of the skies, wheeling and diving until it finally plummeted and was lost in the valleys below. In one effortless flight, thought Ivan with envy, it could have passed the White Fawn and soared to the summit, knowing nothing of the toil which they themselves faced as they struggled onwards, aware only of the buffeting, teasing wind and the growing intensity of the cold.

Ivan lost all track of time as they laboured upwards. Darkness began to fall. Again the wind abated, and as they rested once more the old man began to point out to the boy the stars which he loved. 'There is Aradon', he said, 'which some say was once a maiden; and near her Merilondes, the brightest star, which lights the heavens with its golden glow – its name means Dreambringer'. They looked above them, and could just make out the silhouette of the Fawn poised on a cliff, the winter snow deep about it. Then on they went again, edging upwards now through the first deep gullies of snow that stretched white and sheer above.

It seemed to Ivan many hours later that the storm resumed its earlier force. The old man was a grey shape in the darkness as he climbed, slowly and painfully, ahead of him. Ivan was himself feeling desperately weary; although fully aware that the going must by now be taxing the old man's strength to the limit, he could not bring himself to suggest that he give up. Suddenly the end came. Falliope, crossing a ledge of gleaming ice that lay directly in their path, slipped and fell backwards with a strangled cry. At once Ivan caught and held him safely; then for a time he let him lie still on the snow. His breath came in laboured gasps. After a time he opened his eyes and smiled wearily: 'I owe you my life, Fawnleader', he whispered, 'and for that I thank you. Yet perhaps you should have allowed me to fall, for I am spent and of no use to you. Now the moment has come as I foretold it – you must go on alone'.

'Never say you are of no use to me', argued the boy. 'Surely I owe you much more than you owe me!' Falliope shook his head; then, seeing that Ivan seemed prepared to remain beside him, he said with great urgency:

'You must go on, my son! Waste no more time with me in my weakness; soon I shall recover enough strength to return to my people. But the quest for the jewel, Fawnleader, that is for you alone'. Still Ivan lingered, reluctant to abandon him, while Falliope continued to insist that he must go on without delay. Finally the boy knelt beside him and said farewell.

'I shall follow the Fawn, Falliope', he said, 'no matter where it leads, and even if I fail in the end. I cannot repay you for all you have done for Kerry and me, except if it could be, perhaps, by fulfilling your dream which is ours also. Goodbye, dear friend'. He could say no more; turning, he began to climb again.

Almost at once it seemed that the storm worsened. The night

had become bitterly cold, and the wind buffeted him unmerci-
fully as he stumbled onwards, higher and higher into the black
emptiness which surrounded the snow-wreathed shoulders of
Mount Gilrene. Sleet blinded his eyes once more; it swept in
icy waves from the heights above, causing him to bend almost
double as he struggled upward, striving only to find strength
for the next step, and the next, and the next.

For a long time he climbed mindlessly, almost forgetting
where he was; he seemed to have been on the mountain for an
eternity. Reality returned when lightning flashed from the sky
in a thousand twisted tongues, and as the whole of the peak
was lit up, etched momentarily with perfect clarity, he saw the
White Fawn stepping sure-footed over the beetling rocks high
above; each splintered crag, too, could be clearly seen, and the
ledges that led at last to the great pinnacle of stone that marked
the summit.

Then the heavens seemed like a battlefield as thunder rolled
like great drums, and prongs of lightning above the peak
illumined every rock and gully. In that same light the Fawn
could again be seen bounding from rock to rock as it climbed
ever higher towards the summit. Numb as he was, stiff and
frozen with the bitter cold, Ivan found himself rallying as he
forced himself to recall the reason for his quest; he reminded
himself of Maria and his other kin in the caves, of his beloved
Kerry, of Falliope who had so fully placed his trust in him.
Briefly he rested, and then went on. Soon he would be on the
last lap of the climb.

Yet it seemed many hours later that he was creeping up, his
feet feebly seeking holds in the stone and his hands grasping
the final ledge with every last ounce of energy he could muster.
At long last he was there, almost at the end of his endurance,
gasping, heaving himself over the edge, finding to his surprise
a mossy plateau rather than the rocky slabs he had expected.
Seeing that the Fawn had moved to the centre of the plateau,
he followed, his heart beating fast; surely now he must be near
the end of his quest?

Thunder rolled again, and then came a brilliant flash which
clearly illumined the entire summit; in its light he saw that
the beast was standing beside a smooth-sided slab which bore

mysterious rune-like markings. Again his heart quickened with
excitement, and in the ensuing darkness he groped his way to
the strange rock. The lightning flashed again, a vivid tongue of
flame that lit the stone with argent light, revealing its every
facet and marking; but of the White Fawn there was now no
sign at all. Again all was darkness; but in the brilliance of the
next flash Ivan caught sight of a stone within the stone, a
gem that gleamed with dazzling radiance. Trembling now, he
allowed his fingers to travel over the rocky surface, feeling
every inch until to his joy he felt the smoothness of the jewel.
It was embedded in the rock. His heart sank; yet immediately
there came the assurance that if indeed he was the Fawnleader,
the one of whom Celroc had spoken long ago, then he had the
power to call out the precious gem from its prison in the rock.
And so it proved: pressing hard with his fingers, he found it
could be removed with ease. It was his! With mounting joy he
turned it round in his hand; and then with a sense of disappointment, he knew not why, he realised it had been broken.
Its form was imperfect. He stood for a few moments, buffeted
still by the storm, uncertain of what to do next, wondering
whether the White Fawn would return. Disappointment again
gave way to jubilation – even if the gem was somehow incom-
plete, it was in his keeping. With what triumph he could now
return to Falliope and his people and what joy would be theirs!

Still Ivan waited, while the storm continued and he wondered
what his next step should be. Realising with a sense of sadness
that he would not see the Fawn again, he carefully placed the
jewel in the bag given to him by Falliope to hold his bread. All
the time his thoughts were of Kerry. How good it would be to
see her again, to show her the gem, to have her at his side once
more as they continued their quest! After all, it was hers as
well; together they would find the way forward until at last
they would confront the Voice.

Tiredness washed over him. He would find a place of shelter
and there wait for the dawn. With infinite care, his hand on
the bag which held the precious stone, he began to retrace his
steps.

Part 2

The Healing of Spring

Chapter 1

The King

The passages Kerry wandered in were long, endless, timeless; she was lost, lost for ever in the depths of the mountain, a prisoner falling deeper and yet deeper into the emptiness of unconsciousness. The pulse of fever beat in her flesh, pounding on and unceasing. At times the walls burst into crimson flames, and she was running and running as the fire pursued her, and then it caught and devoured her, and she writhed in the darkness. Then her world seemed to turn dark and she floated on a dusky sea, watching now for the faintest gleam of light where she might find peace and freedom again. In her dreams, shattered fragments of memories would rise like wraiths to haunt her; now she tramped over endless plains deep in snow, blinded by icy winds; now she bent over an old man in the caves, waiting for him to die. Then she would see Peter lying still in death, and she would cry out in anguish. Then all these faded, leaving her so alone that she wept in the prison of her heart, crying out hopelessly against the darkness, terrified of the whispers of the Voice.

Then, at last, there came as it were the first far-off murmur of spring, a time when the faintest glow seemed to light the dimness of her forlorn soul to call her back, call her away to life and health again, beyond the shadows of her prison. At first she did not know at all what it was that called, as she lay wafted on the tide of fever. She only knew in some strange way that it was true. For a moment the caverns and shadows seemed to shudder, to quake in their very foundations, and to weaken as if a tremor of light had come and broken into a hundred filaments of silver thread beneath them. Then the light was gone, and despair washed over her as she had never before

known it, and she felt there could be no more light left in the
world, no glow to guide her and lead her back from the caverns
of silence and death. She was washed away on the edge of the
empty tide. Much later, as she seemed to lift and fall at the
mercy of the waves, she heard the call again, tugging at the
ragged edges of her soul and summoning her to come back,
come back. She tried at first to turn away, to shut out the hope
of return lest she fall deeper still into the silence and emptiness;
yet there came a time when she yearned to follow the call and
find the light again.

It seemed a hopeless struggle, there in the arid desert of her
heart amid the burning heat of fever, yet she stumbled back,
step after step, out of the prison of death, out of the empty
land. She heard the call again so clearly, a single musical note
that echoed and rang like some resonance from a bell struck
long ago, a sound that filled her ears and mind and soul at last
like the rushing of a hundred streams. She must follow! There
could be no turning back for her now; the darkness of death
was behind her, the hope and light of life before. If only she
could rise above the fever, if only she could climb from the tide
of darkness that still engulfed her!

And then she awoke and found that the blackness had caught
her once more, that the illusion of light and life had been only
a dream after all, that death had triumphed. She closed her
eyes, and for a moment it seemed that in her deep sadness she
could only sink back and allow the dark tide to wash over her
and drown her. Yet there was in that dim, dusky light a cool
freshness that she sensed beyond all the hopeless nightmares
and fears, some scent of life and light that again brought her
back, made her open her eyes and begin to fight her stumbling
way to consciousness. The ebony blackness finally left her, and
she became aware that she lay in the warmth of a soft, skin-
covered bed: the waves died away and the noise of their endless
ebb and flow was gone. She caught instead the sound of a wind
that whispered far away, like a gentle breath. Strength seemed
to be flowing back into her limbs. In the distance she still heard
the echoes of the call that had brought her back from the brink
of death, and as she began to move her limbs she felt the
warmth of moss between her toes.

The place in which she found herself was utterly silent. No sound at all could be heard save the echoes of the musical note, and the whisper of the quiet wind that rose and fell. She stumbled with weakness as she rose slowly to her feet, wincing a little with the pain still remaining after the long hours of toiling over the icy plains. Nothing was visible beyond the outline of a door. Passing through the door, she stepped blissfully over the carpet of moss which smelled so sweet in the darkness. It might have been a dream, this strange walk, this waking while she still burned with fever, yet her senses were alert, every sound and scent sharp and clear.

She stood for a moment outside the door of what she now saw was a small wooden hut, and looked up to the night sky. She saw the moon, and a million stars that gleamed like gems. She shivered then as her eyes scanned the empty darkness, and felt a delicious thrill pass over her body, as if a fresh breeze touched her, cooling her fever and setting her free again. Below the clustered stars she saw the silhouettes of the pines, silent ranks of living trees whose branches were silver in the moon's lustre, whose scent of resin was strong in her nostrils. And all the world seemed still and empty; only the branches rustled softly in the whisper of the night wind.

Kerry walked slowly at first beneath the trees, feeling the deep warmth of the needles gratefully under her feet, watching the argent light as it flickered and danced through the branches of the pines above. She followed the call which had awakened her and led her back from the darkness, a call that was somehow full of the glory of rebirth, of spring returned. She did not know why she should feel thus. But it seemed to her from time to time as she walked that she caught a faint glimpse of one who held a horn, and that she heard the sound of his joyous laughter echoing among the still trees; sometimes she fancied that someone called her name, summoning her to follow, drawing her on deeper and further into the forest.

Her steps began to quicken as she glimpsed his shadow as he stopped for a moment by the edge of a silver-lit pool; sometimes she caught a snatch of the melody he played, a skein of rippling notes that seemed to run and play among the trees like a band of unseen children. The snow was melting under her feet, and great drops of water fell from the branches; in the distance she could hear the sound of streams running. It was as if spring itself had burst open, like a bud buried beneath the weight of winter; resurrection had begun, and things which had been dead were coming to life even as she was herself, conquering the will of the Voice who had decreed the deadness.

At last the sound of many waters seemed almost to drown out the sound of the music, so that her heart was saddened, and she feared he might have gone on and left her, or perhaps that he had been no more than a dream. And then with a lift of the heart she saw him, and hurried with all her might to reach him, and came before him with both joy and fear.

And as his face turned towards her, a face radiant with the glory of the spring that was his alone, full of the life that ran within him like a living stream, she looked at him and felt all at once the meanness and unworthiness of her own self. Her eyes dropped before his, and in shame she turned away; she was not fit to see this King. 'No, my daughter,' he said softly, 'do not feel dread in my presence. It was surely right that you should meet with me here, for have I not healed you?' Then as she looked, daring at last to meet the smiling eyes, she knew that indeed it was true, that the fever and the darkness of death were quite gone from her.

'You have seen me, my child', he said, 'because there is much beauty in this land, and because you will not see it for much longer. Ivan, your friend, I have called from the caves of his people to be the Fawnleader, the one who will be used to restore Pyrus and bring the land to the fullest brilliance of a new spring; yet I brought you also, my daughter. Were not you also called?' As he spoke, he gently touched her brow as a tender father might have done, always with a smile of love in his eyes. And when he spoke again it seemed to Kerry as if his voice was strong as with the power of wind and lightning, carrying through the moonlit glades like the cry of the eagle, as it glides and swoops high above the world. 'Come, Kerry, run with me until you can run no more, run until your heart is bursting and you are strong again! Let spring return and flood your heart!'

Then he was gone, faster it seemed than the mightiest steed,

more filled with grace than the purest deer, on and on through
the moonlit night. And, unheeding, Kerry plunged after him
into the argent glory; all time had ceased; in all the world there
was nobody but him, with herself running after him by the
new streams, by the tall trees with their haunting fragrance.
She knew that he could have chosen to vanish into the night –
yet had he not called her, had he not all the beauty of Pyrus to
show her? And so he led her on, always running a little before
her, drawing her onwards, deeper and deeper into the forest.
And she ran as if her strength would never fail, laughing as if
a spring of life welled within her, as if there never had been a
fever, never the dark shadow of death. He was leading her,
too, far from the caverns of fear in her own heart, further and
deeper into the true land, the real Pyrus where the Voice could
never come. Her soul sang within her.

By silver paths he led her, by ways that passed the snow-
filled brooks and were still white with the ice of former days,
through valleys where the trees formed stately avenues, lit by
the mellow radiance of the moon. Time itself seemed to have
ceased. She knew nothing but that of all things she wanted
only to be near him; all else was false, and had no meaning.

At last the rushing streams seemed to run more fiercely;
the brooks were flecked with foam, and the silver plumes of
waterfalls cascaded from the rock walls. They were descending
from the hills to a wide valley, a place where a great river
wound and carved its way through the plains. They reached at
last the banks of this river, where a hundred brooks met,
melded to become one, the Elidon, Stream of the Deer. As he
stood before her, the King did not at once turn towards her;
instead, he faced the silver cascades as they rushed from the
heights above. Then, even above the sound of the waters, she
heard with joy his own song. It seemed to her that the very
trees bowed nearer to him to hear the melody; and then as she
watched, she saw him beckon to her. His face appeared to her
brighter than any star, purer, gentler, more loving than anything she could have imagined. She found herself half-stumbling over the moon-dappled grass, her eyes almost closed
because of the radiance of his countenance; but she went to his
side, to the very edge of the river, which wound like a great

silver plume among the pines, full of the violent turbulence of the many streams which fed it. He held up his hand, and then, looking away from her again, stood tall above the water, full of might and power.

'Be still,' he said, 'Hold back the violence of your strength!' His voice was a command: it reached out over the first furious reaches of the river, and past them to the cascades of tumbling water. For a moment there was heard his command, loud even above the chaos of that confluence, a voice both sure and strong; then only silence, with the waters still and the night deathly calm. The waters were turned back; there was left where the first cascades had been only a deep rounded pool, a place where the moonlight now danced and played.

Nothing else could be heard save the haunting whispers of the pines, and the sound of the King's voice which rose and fell, singing once more, only his song had become a hymn that told of spring, that bore away the last vestiges of winter's power. Yet the song had changed also; now it told of resurrection and replenished spirit, of peace and harmony between man and beast, of the healing of a rift which had endured too long. It was an invocation, a calling back of the beasts which had turned their backs on man and ignored his commands, which had turned to the darkness of the forests. His song pleaded with them, reached out into the emptiness of the endless pines, called them to return once more, to drink from the waters of the new spring. Then his voice faltered.

Kerry looked up at him, standing still over the waters. His head was bowed and his song died away. 'I wanted to call them back, Kerry,' he said. 'I wanted the deer to return and live at peace again, yet they will not answer. I shall call them one last time, as on the day I mustered and named them. They must on no account be lost.'

He went forward and she saw him standing, his robe fluttering in the breath of the wind. And then he began to sing again, the hymn that had not been sung since the first morning of creation, when the new sun had risen above the furthest mountains in the east, when the trees and flowers had been born from the earth, when the streams and rivers had first run in Pyrus. And as he sang, as he uttered the psalm of summoning by the edge of the silent waters, the moon illumined the tears on his face. When he had ceased, he called out a single word.

For a long time nothing was heard, only the echo of his cry and the sound of the wind in the pines. At last, in the deepest shadows of the forest, there was a stirring, a kind of rumour of noise among the pines. And then they came forth, beast after noble beast, heads silver and dappled bright in the shimmering glory of the moonlight, breaths steaming in the ebony of the night, hooves soft and gentle on the carpet of needles beneath them. Only then did the King lift his head again and cry for joy, throwing his arms wide in welcome and laughing like a child as they came one by one from the high slopes to drink from the silver pool. There were tiny fawns among them, still frail and tottering as they came from the shadows and bowed their heads at the margin of the pool. All drank at the place which he had made for them, a place of stillness where the waters rushed and roared no more. And when they were done, when they had drunk their fill of the waters of the Elidon, when they had obeyed the call of the King who once had named them and who had returned to forge anew the bond between his people and their own, they raised their heads and stood quite still.

The girl did not understand why they should linger there now that the call of the King had been answered; nor did she understand his look of joy and youthfulness as he beckoned for her to come to him. 'Come,' he said gently. 'We must show them that our love is strong. We must forge a new bond between man and beast, a bond that will endure until all things are ended and there is peace at last. Come, Kerry, come and drink from the waters of spring.'

She felt that her legs would not bear her, that she could not walk these few steps to his side as he waited for her, smiling, at the edge of the pool. Then she dropped to her knees beside him on the cold shingle, cupped the icy water in her hands and tasted it again and again.

When she rose it was as if she had wakened from a deep sleep, as if she had been drawn from an endless darkness, out into the brightness of the moonlight, into the healing of spring. Tears brimmed in her eyes, yet she did not weep; she was smiling and laughing as she looked at his face. She was rejoicing because this was what she had always longed for, the fulfilment of her deepest dreams. Her life, she felt now, had been itself like winter; she had been as it were tossed by tempests, tortured by the menace of the Voice, trapped and wandering in a hollow mountain within her own bitter heart, and calling, always calling for her own lost self. To see Pyrus under the glory of the sun – as she had dreamed of doing – was as nothing, was useless while the Voice still held her people in thrall; but this, this was what her soul had really been seeking, this was the balm that would heal all wounds. Her whole heart was given to this King! It was not merely that she had drunk from the pool; she was aware that she had sipped new life, had tasted the fountain of spring, the waters the King alone could give, which alone could bring healing.

This was why she laughed, laughed along with him, as he stood tall beside her in the moonlight; she felt she had been set free, that there were no more tears to be cried, no more darkness to be endured. She had walked in the bleakness of winter, and like a child had searched the dark caverns for the light that would lead her back; yet perhaps in her heart she had known that she would never find it, that it could only be given.

'You want all darkness to end, Kerry', he said, and his voice was full of tenderness and love, with no hint of reproach. 'Yet it cannot be so for you – not yet, my child. I have given you light that the darkness may be easier to bear when it comes, and that will not be long now. You have tasted life, the true life, the life that makes a hollow mockery of that which you have known till now; and you seek to make it your own. Do not think I scold you for seeking the one thing which cannot yet be granted to you. I have allowed you this taste of life because I know that death and darkness are still before you, and because I can draw aside the curtain and show you only the smallest fragment of the light that is my own. I would have you remember one thing, Kerry – death is not the end!'

He was quiet then and she saw that his face was sad. 'Now I will take you a little way', he said at last, 'and while you walked behind me when first you came, now you must go ahead of me to the place where I will leave you gently, as a father who sees and knows his daughter's every step, yet cannot save her from the pain she alone must bear. So come, my Kerry! See, the fawns have left us: there is no more to do'. Once more he smiled at her, the King, the one who knew her as no other ever had, the one who had forgiven her and given her the gift of new life. A wave of sadness threatened to overwhelm her.

In the midst of her grief she saw him turn again to the waters which his own command had earlier caused to be still. Then he held his hand high and called one word, 'Serendon!', and the waters tumbled again from the rocks; the roar of the cataracts returned. The King beckoned to her then to walk in front of him, and although he spoke no word to her, she knew that he had said farewell. She walked slowly for a little way, then turned, knowing that he was gone. For a long time she stood lost in thought, looking and looking at the place where he had been. Already the meeting had begun to seem like a dream. At last she turned away, and began to make her way back to the people of Pyrus.

Chapter 2

Return

Ivan knew that he must be nearing Falliope's village in the forest when he smelt the wood fires. His heart quickened, and his steps became lighter; soon he would see Kerry again! He hardly dared believe that she would be well; even if she had regained consciousness, that would be joy enough for him. He imagined himself showing her the jewel. Then his joy clouded again; what if, after all, she had died? He thrust the thought away, and began instead to picture Falliope's excitement at the sight of the gem. Even in this there was a shadow of uncertainty – what if the old man had not had sufficient strength to make his way home? And the stone itself – why was it broken? From the start this had puzzled him; yet he did know with certainty that he had found all of it that lay in the rock on Mount Gilrene. Perhaps the people of Pyrus would help to solve the mystery. He walked on, savouring the resinous aroma of the pines.

Then, as he entered a long avenue, his heart turned over. Far down the path, under the trees, a slight figure was stooping – Kerry! He began to run, all the while telling himself he must be mistaken; even if she had recovered, it was impossible, unthinkable, that she should so soon be out in the forest. Yet his heart told him it was true; unbelievably, it was his dear Kerry. She straightened as he came near, and he saw that she had been picking flowers. Then she saw him and began to run towards him, her arms held wide. 'Ivan, oh Ivan!' she cried in utter joy, and they were holding each other close, laughing and crying together, and then standing back so that each could look at the other.

'Did the Fawn lead you . . . did you find the stone?', she burst out at once. For reply he opened the small bag and held up the dark shining gem. Reverently she took it and looked long at it, saying nothing at first. It gleamed in the sunlight; she noticed its strange shape, but said nothing. Then she held him close again and cried 'You have conquered, Fawnleader! How proud I am of you!'

'Why do you call me that, Kerry?' he asked quietly.

'It is the name Falliope and his people call you', she replied, 'and it is rightly yours.'

'The old man,' he asked next,'is he well again? I had to leave him on the mountain and go on alone'.

'I know, Ivan,' she answered. 'He was exhausted when he came home; now he is resting, but I have seen him and he is recovering'.

'But we talk of recovery, Kerry', said Ivan, looking at her almost in disbelief. 'You are the one who has recovered – oh, I can hardly believe it! I could not trust my eyes when I caught sight of you, and yet from the first glimpse I knew it was you – how could I ever mistake you? The story of the jewel can wait; tell me, tell me now how it is that you are well again? You look . . . you look like a new person!'

For a moment Kerry did not reply. How was she to explain to him that she had met the King? Would he ever understand what had happened to her, that she was indeed a new person, that she had tasted the healing of spring? Ivan, growing impatient, said again, 'Tell me how it is that you are well – surely the people of Pyrus are indeed able physicians?'

'Not the people of Pyrus, Ivan', she said softly, 'although indeed they treated me with much kindness. But when you were gone, I met the King, and he healed me. I had a fever, and was near to death, but he healed me in a moment'.

'The king of Pyrus?' he asked, uncomprehending.

'Not the king of Pyrus, Ivan, or even of that other world where we should have lived, but the King of life, the one who can call the seasons and command the rivers, and bring the beasts from their hiding-places'.

Her eyes were alight now, her face bright with a radiance he could not comprehend, a joy he had never seen there before – indeed it came to him that he had never before seen Kerry's face without a look of sadness. Now she seemed almost to be basking in the glory of some wonderful new hope. All at once a spasm of pain pierced his soul; his Kerry, his very own dear friend, had given her heart to this King! Never again would she truly belong to him!

Unaware of the turmoil of his thought, the girl was continuing: 'It seems so long ago already, Ivan – I awoke in the darkness, and even from the depths of the fever I somehow knew he was calling me, and I must follow', she explained. 'I had to find him! I must have followed for quite a long time, through the pines and past the streams, until he led me to a much greater river, flowing far away through the wood.' Haltingly at times, yet always with the same glowing look, she went on to describe as best she could her meeting with the King, his stilling of the waters, the calling forth of the beasts, her drinking of the water of life.

At last the boy interrupted: 'But Kerry, if he really was the King of all life, were you not afraid in his presence?' She was silent as she pondered his question.

'Although he is the King, Ivan', she replied slowly, 'and power and majesty seem to flow from him, yet at the same time he is . . . he is all love; he takes away your fear. No, after the first moment I was not afraid – only ashamed'.

'You, Kerry, ashamed?' he burst out in genuine bewilderment, 'surely you of all people have nothing to be ashamed of?'

'Quietly', she answered, 'how can I possibly explain to you what he is like? It is as if when he looks at you, he sees at once all the meanness of your soul! And yet he forgives.' He looked at her shining eyes, and again a stab of pain went through him. 'But, Ivan,' cried Kerry then, 'I have been telling you all that has happened to me, but I have heard almost nothing of how you followed the White Fawn and found the stone!'

Ivan shook his head. 'Not now, Kerry,' he said. 'That story must wait. We must not keep Falliope waiting any longer – he deserves to see the jewel he has awaited all his life! Come, let us find him now.' Hand in hand they went running down the woodland path and soon reached Falliope's hut.

The old man was sitting outside in the sunshine; he recognised them at once and called out, smiling eagerly: 'Fawnleader! Have you conquered? Have you found the jewel?' For answer,

Ivan opened the bag and laid the precious stone in his hand, where it lay gleaming, catching the rays of the sun. 'Ah,' the old man breathed, turning it over and over with a look of awed wonder on his face. His fingers felt the cut edge and he murmured as if to himself: 'So they were right . . . a riven stone.' And then to Ivan: 'It is not a complete gem, my son.'

'No,' the boy replied, 'I noticed its strange shape at once, and I have been uneasy ever since because of it. All I know is that this is what the White Fawn led me to – there was nothing more.'

'Ah, Fawnleader, I should have told you the legend,' answered Falliope. 'The story has been repeated all down the generations of my people that the stone of which Celroc spoke was broken – as they say, riven by the Voice in order to free himself. Nobody knows what this means, and in Celroc's prophecy there was no word of it. So I have never believed it, and I would not tell you of it before you left on your quest. I was wrong, my son; forgive a stubborn old man.'

Ivan was silent for a few moments as he pondered what this might mean; Kerry too was quiet. Then the boy asked: 'What do you think it means – that there is another part still to be found?'

'That is indeed what they say', was the reply, 'and that the other part must be found to make it whole, before the Voice can be destroyed'. Ivan's heart sank: if one part of the ancient story had been proved true, surely it must all be true? Then he had only just begun his quest!

'Come, my friend, do not look so sad', said Falliope. 'You have done well; already half the victory has been won and our land will soon be free again. Tonight we shall rejoice together, for all my people will wish to prepare a feast for you! We are poor, but we shall share the best we have with our honoured guests.'

Before long the two young people were sitting among a glad company round a great fire, and as the food was passed to them, Ivan whispered to the girl: 'Do you realise, Kerry, that never in our lives have we had more food than we wanted? Indeed, we have been hungry most of the time'.

'And Ivan', added Kerry, 'nobody ever sang in the caves!' –

for now the people of Pyrus were singing, singing in the tongue of the men who once laid the foundations of a great city, a city which now was no more. It was a haunting melody, and the people sang with great sweetness, so that the two were transported with delight, and had no words in which to express their thanks.

Much later, when Falliope and his folk had gone to rest, they sat together in the moonlight under the sweet-smelling pines. Both were aware that tomorrow they must take their leave and go on with their journey towards the kingdom of the Voice. A dark shadow lay on each of their hearts. Ivan was deeply apprehensive because of the broken jewel: how, he wondered, would the other part ever be found; would it be in the keeping of the Voice himself? If so, surely the quest was impossible. Yet what choice could there be? Had they not known in their hearts that they must leave the caves, and one day face the malignant power of the Voice, no matter what the cost might be? Nothing had changed; they must still face him; and was it not reasonable to trust that even as the White Fawn had led the way to one part of the stone, so in some way as yet unknown would the other part be found? So he reasoned within himself. Then, weary with trying to puzzle out the mystery, he turned to Kerry and began at last to recount the story of his ascent of Mount Gilrene.

She listened with rapt attention, saying nothing until he had finished; then she took both his hands in hers and said: 'Oh Ivan, you are indeed the Fawnleader – how proud Maria would be if she knew!' He made no reply, but returned the pressure of her hands. She was well aware that his thoughts were often with Maria, although he seldom spoke of her. As for her, no day passed without memories of Peter, and many times in dreams he came to her.

They moved to a clearing so as to watch the stars. Kerry was wrestling with the dark shadow which had so soon taken away the fullness of her joy after meeting the King: now the message of impending death which he had brought to her lay heavy on her heart. She was afraid. Remembering the healing of the waters, the smile of the King, the intensity of her feeling of release on the night when she met him, she marvelled that in so short a time she could feel fear again, and was ashamed. At times the old joy would well up to drown the fear; then the shadow would fall once more.

She knew that she should share this fear with Ivan, should tell him all that the King had said; yet she could not. Already instinct told her that Ivan, dear friend as he was, could not be expected to share her feelings about the King. If only he could have met him too! Then he would have tasted new life as well. But the news that she was soon to die – how could she tell him? He would be desolate; or perhaps he would altogether reject it. In any case she could not tell him tonight; this was a night of peace, perhaps indeed their last, among the kindly people who had comforted them and shared with them their food and their songs. Tomorrow, once they had set out again on their journey, she would tell him all that the King had said.

Chapter 3

The Shadow

Falliope and some of his people accompanied the two young travellers for the first part of the way. The old leader had provided food for their journey, and then spent some time explaining the way they must take in order to find the ruins of the ancient city of Pyrus: even as he spoke, however, Ivan was conscious that he already knew the way, and a spasm of foreboding crossed his heart.

Now the time had come to say farewell. The old man stood tall and stately on the hillside with his folk around him. 'My friends', he said in his resonant voice, 'there are no words great enough to thank you for what you have done for me and my people! Listen to the streams as they rush with their winter load to the sea; hear the sighing of the trees as their branches revel in the breezes of spring, freed at last from the curse of the endless storms of winter. Celroc's horn has been blown, the jewel has been found, and the fawns have already welcomed the one for whom they waited so long. Soon the fetters that bind our land will be broken forever!'

Listening to his words, Ivan wished fervently that he could share his high hopes. Kerry, looking at him, saw him like a statue, old and rugged, as if carved from marble and left as a timeless prophet to cry out his visions to any who would hear. He was speaking again: 'One thing I ask of you, friends, as you leave us and go towards the west, over the waters of the Reed Lands, that you seek beyond them the ruins of Pyrus, the great city that once was, and that surely will be again one day. When you have found it, search diligently in its heart for the torch of the Eternal Flame (for when you find it you will easily recognise it). It is the brand that was to burn until the Voice had gained full dominion in our land, until the last of our peoples had been enslaved. Each day, each moment is precious in this our time of freedom; and although till now we have dreaded that the last shadow would not be long in falling, now we have a new hope. By the burning brand you will know that we still live! And so farewell, dear children, and may you not fail to carry out that which remains to be done. Farewell!'

A chorus of valediction echoed all around them, and then Ivan and Kerry, having poured out their own heartfelt thanks, turned away sad at heart. As they went, the people began again to sing the song of Pyrus, their clear voices rising high above the sighing of the wind. The haunting song receded further and further until only the faintest sound could be heard. Neither Ivan nor Kerry looked back, and no words were spoken for a long time. Then the boy said quietly: 'Their singing is gone now, but I shall hear it in my dreams, haunting me. They are depending on us, Kerry – what if we should fail them?' She herself could find no words to reassure him, and said nothing. Suddenly he left her side and plunged downwards below the shadow of the pines; there she would not see his tears.

It seemed many hours later that they came to the crest of the hillside and saw far beneath them the foam-flecked streams plunging downwards to be swallowed in the mighty Elidon. Then the memories of the night when she met the King returned to Kerry with vivid clarity. She saw his face, recalled the stillness of the mighty cataract after he had issued his kingly command, watched in memory the graceful deer with their fawns as they drank from the moonlit waters of the pool, felt the grief of his farewell. More memories flooded back to her, bringing her again the moment when he led her to the edge of the water and bade her drink. And now the remembrance returned of the new life that had come to her; she tasted afresh in memory the pure water, and knew again as surely as she had before that she was healed, she was renewed, and nothing for her would ever be the same again. But even in the joy of her remembering there came a return of a dark shadow that loomed above her, seeming to her like the black wings of a raven which shut the light out from her soul. Unaware that she spoke aloud, she suddenly cried out in anguish: 'How can I face it without him beside me?'

Instantly Ivan was at her side, querying anxiously to know what was wrong. 'Ivan', she said earnestly, 'let us sit and rest, and eat some of the food our friends gave us. Then I must tell you more of what the King said to me, for indeed I should have told you before'. Ivan said nothing, but sat with a sinking heart, waiting till she should be ready. Why should his heart always falter at the mention of this King? Why should he feel as if a barrier had been set between them, that there was a part of her lost to him? Then she was speaking in a quiet but resolute voice. 'Look down there, Ivan', she said, 'there is the great river, the Elidon, where he gave me the water that was like the water of life itself! It was there he told me he had called you to be the Fawnleader – and should not that give you new hope? – and he said he had called me too. Then I knew you had truly been chosen to save the Unborn, and to destroy the Voice! But there is more, I confess – and you must not allow this to lie too heavily on your heart – he said that he was showing me this beauty because I would not see it for much longer, that he was giving me life to fight against darkness and death, for the darkness would not be long in coming to cover me. And I found I was ready to bear his words and to conquer the fear because of the courage which came to me from him. But now . . . Ivan, I have to confess that despite this, fear sometimes overwhelms me!'

Ivan had not taken his eyes from her face while she spoke, nor moved at all: now he suddenly lunged forward, grasped her shoulders and pulled her round to face him. His eyes blazed with a mixture of anger and grief; for the first time in her life, she could almost have been afraid of him. 'Is that all the value you place on your life?' he almost shouted; 'did you leave the caves with me and brave the meeting with the Priests and struggle through the snow and ice to give up your freedom now? Oh Kerry, Kerry, have I never told you that I love you? Did I not carry you in my arms over the plains, desperate for your safety? Is that all you value my love? And this King you talk of – have you not given your love to him instead?'

'Oh Ivan', she replied, searching for the right words, 'I can understand your grief, but you are so wrong in this – how can I explain that to give my love to the King does not mean that I give less to you! Of course I know you love me; I know too that your courage saved my life. But because the King . . . the King is the source of all love, it seems to me that loving him means I have even more love, not less, to give to you'.

He was silent for a few moments and then, his anger past, he held her in his arms, his face pale and tense, tears streaking his cheeks. 'I spoke wrongly', he then said gently, stroking her soft hair and kissing her brow as he might a child's. 'You mean everything to me, Kerry. You are father and mother, sister and brother; you are my dear and only love. Try to see that I cannot imagine life without you – if you were to leave me, I would be utterly alone! Yes, I admit I am selfish, greedy for your love. And I was jealous of your love for this King. But I shall try to understand all that you say about him'. He was lost in thought then, and finally said slowly: 'What I do not understand is why, if he really is the King of life, he cannot save you from this death he has predicted'.

'Nor do I understand', replied the girl, 'and oh, Ivan, how I wish it did not have to be so! I only know that somehow he expected me to accept it and draw courage from him; but he could not, or perhaps would not, save me from it. What makes me so ashamed is my fear – I feel I have failed him already!'

'Kerry', he said then, and all anger was gone from his voice, and she heard only love in his words, 'I was given the power to summon the White Fawn, and later, when I had climbed to the Mount of the Eagles, to prize this jewel from the rock at its summit. Yet it was you who drew me from the caves when the Voice would have bewitched me to draw me back! Do not say that you lack courage; you gave me courage to keep on, in that misery of cold and tiredness. Without you I would be lost, after you have come so far as my companion! It would be hard, so very hard for me to go on alone to meet the Voice!' Overcome again with grief, he let his head rest in his hands.

Pity for him washed over her. 'No, Ivan, Fawnleader, dear friend and companion', she said softly, 'it is you who have given me the courage to come thus far, you who led me and gave me hope and light when there was nothing but emptiness in my heart. And it is I who ask forgiveness for the many times when I would gladly have lain down in the snow and given up the struggle; it was your strength of will, your courage which carried me to safety in spite of all the hardships. It is so very hard to say this, Ivan, but I must say it: I know in my heart the truth of the King's words, that the darkness is coming closer, and indeed I have felt its shadow, like that of some great black bird' – she shuddered as she spoke – 'approaching for a long time now. Yet I am torn between two things – between my desire to be with you and live at last in a land freed from the evil power of the Voice, and going to that place which I have seen in my dreams, a land of sunshine and joy and laughter. Oh, if only you knew how hard it is! If only you could see as I can see the country beyond us! But I will stay until the King calls me; I promise I will be at your side. Do not make it harder for me, dear one; our love will be strong to the end. Do you know what the King's last words to me were? "I would have you remember one thing – death is not the end" '.

He did not reply, and when she looked again she saw that he was holding the jewel, turning it in his hand. He held it up to the light, and it seemed to burn with some hidden flame; for the first time she saw its facets sparkle, the heart of it dark as ebony. Suddenly he stood up, the gem still in his hand. A stream ran below where they had stopped, and as he raised his hand, she realised that he was about to hurl it into the water. She found herself lunging towards him; then his arm dropped to his side. He seemed to come to himself then, and asked her forgiveness. 'But what good is it to me, Kerry?', he asked in anguish. 'How can I live on in this land if you are no longer by my side? It would mean nothing – nothing, I tell you!' Desolate, he sat with his head buried in his hands.

In a few moments he rose, and they began to walk on again, Ivan going a little way ahead as if he wished to be left alone with his thoughts. Kerry understood, and made no attempt to follow too closely; in any case she too wanted to be alone – so many questions pressed upon her. Ivan, she knew, had tried to dispel her feelings of shame over her fear, but she was not consoled. How was it that she could be at one time filled with joy at the memory of the King and his love, and yet so soon be plunged into sadness and foreboding by the approach of the shadow? If only she could see the King's face again! And yet, should she not be deeply grateful that she had indeed seen him – surely a privilege granted to few? How sad her lack of trust must make him! She walked on, seeing nothing of the beauty around, even forgetting Ivan in the intensity of her emotions.

Suddenly she became aware that Ivan was surrounded by a whole herd of animals: the deer had come out of the forest and down the hillside to gather round the Fawnleader! Perhaps, she thought in wonder, they had somehow perceived that the one whose coming they had long awaited was near to leaving them, and had come to bid him farewell. The boy turned to her as she approached, and pointed delightedly to the small fawns flocking around him; they nuzzled and rubbed against him fearlessly, seeming to take pleasure in his caresses. His face was transformed; he looked fulfilled, joyful, every inch their Fawnleader, and he beckoned to Kerry to come and stand by his side. She would fain have done so, and caressed them too, but to her sadness they shrank from her. Again and again she stretched out her hands to them, but always they turned away. 'They love you only, Ivan', she said then; 'they know their Fawnleader'.

'I am sorry, Kerry', he said simply. 'I know you would love them too. One day they will know and trust you!' As quickly as they had come, they left his side and soon were mere specks on the hillside above, and the two felt a sense of loss at their going.

Kerry was aware in that moment that their trust had given solace and new strength to her companion. She perceived in him a renewed determination; even his step seemed stronger and more assured. At first no words passed between them; then he stopped and took her hands. 'Again I ask you to forgive me, my Kerry', he said in a low voice.

'But why? There is nothing to forgive', she replied.

'Kerry, I confess that the prospect of losing you destroyed all my courage and hope', he insisted. 'I was ready to give up the quest – indeed I had for the time forgotten even Maria and Peter and all the Unborn, as well as Falliope and all our other good friends, friends who are relying on us as their only hope.

How could I be so selfish and cowardly? My heart still quails at the thought of what it would mean to be left alone – indeed I dare not even imagine it. But the coming of the fawns . . . their trust in me brought back the memory of all I had promised, all the determination I once had to destroy the Voice and set this land free! That is all, Kerry. Forgive me'. For answer she held him close.

As the daylight went and the skies slowly became a blue-black canopy above them, they came to the edge of the Woods of Fall, a place that stands high above the lands in the west. They stood side by side looking at all the beauty stretched before them, and at that moment the moon came from behind the clouds to light the Falls of Belimine, the falls that plunged into the waters of the Elidon, flowing into the Reed Lands. Somewhere out there, they surmised, must lie the ruins of the ancient city of Pyrus, long since destroyed by the flames of the Priests. And yet, as long as the single fire of the Eternal Flame was kindled, they would know that some of the people of the land still lived.

Then on they went, weary now, westwards by the banks of the great Elidon, for Kerry a river never to be forgotten. In the darkness Ivan led Kerry by a stony path, where the thunder of the Falls of Belimine was loud in their ears. And at last they reached a place where the Falls plummeted to a circular pool, and then fell in seven steps to the flat and empty Reed Lands. There the grass was deep and soft. Wrapped in their warm cloaks, they lay down to sleep like tired children. The girl saw that her companion fell asleep at once. For her, sleep was long in coming; still she fought to retain the new life and hope given her by the King; still the deepening darkness pursued her. When at last she drifted into a light and troubled sleep, it was as if the two states of her mind fought together for mastery even in dreams, for while she saw again the radiant form of the King standing by the stilled waters, yet she awoke sweating with fear as the huge black wings of a bird hovered over her head.

Chapter 4

The Reed Lands

Kerry awoke to find Ivan lying back in the sunlight watching her. He was smiling; then, seeing that something troubled her, he came over to her and gently touched her face. 'You have had bad dreams', he said quietly.

'It was the Voice, Ivan', she told him. 'And I keep hearing him speak, over and over again, telling me of the shadow that was coming nearer. And then I saw the shadow – it kept coming closer and I ran and ran, until at last I looked back and it was only a bird!' She laughed emptily, but her eyes shimmered with tears, and the look of terror in them betrayed her; dark rings of sleeplessness were visible in the morning light. 'I can't hold on much longer, Ivan!' she said then. 'I'm losing the light. Each day it goes a little more; each day the shadow moves closer. Don't let me go! Don't let me be alone!'

The tears now streamed down her cheeks. She was pleading with him, pleading for she knew not what: it seemed as if nothing but darkness was left. Even the King seemed like someone seen in a dream. For answer the boy smiled at her in love and caught her hands, swinging her up to stand by him, and then kissing away her tears. 'Forget the night', he said, and his voice was full of a new buoyancy and a deep love for her, a love that knew no bounds, no reservations. 'That was only a dream, dear Kerry; the shadow has not come. We are still here together, and it is a new day. See how beautiful it is! Let us enjoy this day together!' His buoyant mood cheered her; for the moment at least she forgot her fears.

They shared some bread together and went to drink from the river. She bent down and drank the cold water of the falls, and as she drank greedily, she felt as if new life and strength flowed into her, even though she was aware that had she drained all the rivers of Pyrus, nothing would have changed. And then the memory of the golden land returned once more and she seemed to see again the King's face, below the pines in the silver moonlight. She would hold on to that picture, she told herself; come what might, she would not allow the Voice to defeat her; she belonged to the King.

Down they went into the broad fields of Pyrus, into the lands where Celroc once led his people. Never before had Ivan been so conscious of the beauty around him, never before felt so strongly the urge to set Pyrus free from the dark oppression under which it had laboured for so long. Time in its every beat was precious. Suddenly he was acutely aware of the approach of darkness; the forest would be the next to be conquered, with the last of Celroc's kin; the fawns would be slain and evil would reign supreme. It was life or death – to lose Pyrus for ever, or to conquer the hated Voice. There was no other choice.

It was then that, for the first time in their deprived young lives, they heard the skylarks, pouring out their joyous trilling notes as they rose up ever higher to the glory of the heavens. The travellers watched them, speechless, and to Ivan at least it seemed as if for a time he soared with them, following them in their every drive and plummet. Kerry drank in the beauty of sight and sound which seemed to envelop them. Both walked on with a new lightness of step, hardly noticing where they were going, until they found themselves on a reeded peninsula, at a place where the Woods of Fall came to an end. On the far side ran two channels carved deep into the plain, almost choked with the reeds which crowded there. At that moment he remembered, word for word, the instructions Falliope had carefully given for this part of their journey. 'At one time we sent messengers to the ancient city', he said, 'and my own son was among those who left our forests so that he might bring us word of its fate. By the foam-filled river mouth he found the craft once fashioned by our people, the last coracle left of the myriad boats that went upon the waters when the Voice was yet but an evil rumour. It bore him well, for there is a magic in our craft that holds the sap of branch and bough through countless winters; and he brought word to us again as spring was melting the winter snows'. Falliope had paused for what seemed to Ivan a long time, pained by the bitter memory of the years when his people had been driven deeper and deeper into the refuge of the pines, and when all tidings of Pyrus were lost. 'Still it must lie there', he continued at last, 'the one remaining coracle, if the winter winds have not destroyed it, nor the reeds buried it. I pray that you may find it, and that it may bear you well'.

At first, despite careful searching, there was nothing to be seen. Then, as Kerry leapt across the narrows, she suddenly noticed a place where the bank had fallen away, a place quite hidden from the other shore; there to her joy she caught sight of the wooden prow of a boat half hidden in the reeds. 'Look, Ivan!' she cried excitedly; he joined her at once and the two of them began to strain and tug, working the ancient coracle free from its muddy prison. Then at last it floated clear with all the grace and eagerness of a well-built craft whose timbers are still sound. Eagerly, like children, they clambered in; they laughed in sheer pleasure to see how well it had weathered the years.

'They have even left us an oar!', the boy exulted. A little awkwardly at first, but soon becoming more adept, he began to dig the oar deep into the water and the craft began to move with ease. He laughed again with delight; Kerry too was cheered. Surely there could be no shadow, nothing else but this sunlit land, the larks above, and the gentle splash of water on wood! Her eye caught the azure flash of a kingfisher as it darted among the islands. Westward there seemed to be nothing but a never-ending stretch of emerald land and cerulean blue water; as the eye followed them to the farthest horizon, they melded to become as one great ocean reaching in the emptiness to an unknown shore, a kingdom where perhaps nobody had ever been before. She felt she was moving in a dream. The coracle cut a straight path into the west, regardless of the reeds, sailing strong and true as if with joy in the skill of the men who had once so lovingly shaped it and granted it life.

They lost all track of time; the girl was half asleep, trailing her hand in the water, when Ivan broke the silence: 'Kerry', he said, 'can you remember the last time we sailed over water?'

She was quiet for a moment, then answered, 'I remember, but so dimly – the woman in the canoe'.

'The first day', he murmured, almost as if to himself. 'The first words of kindness before the caves'. He was quiet again for a long time, and then, pointing down into the water where dark shadows played, he stopped and said, 'Look down there: where the dark shadows are, I saw the caves! I had such a strange feeling, as if we were about to enter the dreadful labyrinth again. Oh Kerry, I think I had been beginning to forget . . . but it is true, and they are still there! And we dare not fail the Unborn'. Afterwards he was lost in thought for a long time.

It was the girl who next broke the silence. She spoke diffidently, uncertainly, even although she faced him fully and frankly. 'Ivan', she said quietly, 'do you remember, long ago in the caves, how we once shared the stories Peter and Maria had told us of their parents? And how neither of us could ever bear to tell the other what the Voice had told us of our own?' He nodded, and she continued: 'I have been thinking, Ivan – and perhaps the vivid memory of the caves a little while ago has given me the courage to say it at last – should we not share now what we have known for so long? We are – we are so close to each other now', she faltered. What she did not say, although it was in both their minds, was that this might well be their last chance, their final day together.

He considered for a long moment, and then said, 'You are right, Kerry. Sometimes I too have thought of it, but I lacked your courage'.

Kerry was silent again for a time. She was looking at him, hesitating to begin her story and yet conscious that there had been in his voice such a depth of compassion, of shared grief, that she felt she was at last ready to allow someone else to share that which had been as it were locked in the inner citadel of her being, to breach the barrier beyond which she had never before permitted anyone to come. She spoke softly, but her clear voice easily reached him.

'One night', she began, 'as Peter and I sat by the fire late, he and I told each other all that the Voice had whispered to us. To our surprise, we found the two stories had much in common

– our parents were very poor, and it was because of their poverty and because they already had more children than they could properly provide for that they were advised not to have another'. Her voice faltered; he saw that she was fighting tears. Then she added: 'You remember how Maria always said "the Voice tells us these things only to break our hearts" – he kept on telling us both what happened afterwards to our families; in each there was great unhappiness. Nothing was changed – the poverty was still there'. Again her voice failed her; then she added brokenly: 'Oh Ivan, think what it would have been for them to have a son as fine as Peter!' She was weeping quietly now.

'Think, dear Kerry', he said softly, 'think what your parents missed in not having you!' At once the thought came to him of what life would have been like for him without her; his heart lurched painfully as he realised that any moment she might indeed be snatched away from him. It took him several minutes to summon the courage to begin his own story.

'What the Voice told me is altogether different', he began in a low voice. 'It was my mother who destroyed me'. He used the harsh word deliberately, bitter thoughts of his rejection coming flooding back even as he spoke; but for Maria and Kerry, how could he have borne it? The old agony rose in his heart; fighting for mastery he continued: 'She had spent her youth in a great city, and for her, material things were everything. She had always craved what seemed to her success in life. She was beautiful, and loved to be admired. Then she met my father, and for a time things were different – they were happy, and two little girls were born to them. Then, a few years later, she found she was to have another child. She had vowed to have no more children, and by this time was employed in an important post. There was a sharp quarrel, as my father, a gentle man, pleaded with her to think of their family happiness, and leave her work. But she would not listen. She had me destroyed'. Again he chose to use the harsh word: Kerry scarcely recognised his voice, so hard and full of bitterness it seemed. She looked across at him in love and pity, feeling along with him the sense of rejection. 'That is not all', he went on. 'Soon after, she left home – left my father and two sisters, and never returned'. The girl could find no words; she simply touched his hand gently in sympathy. 'Her name was Celia', he added as an afterthought. They were quiet again for a time, and then the boy burst out: 'How can you be so calm, Kerry? Do you feel no bitterness? Do you not suffer the terrible pain of rejection?'

'For years I have felt it, Ivan', she replied. 'For me perhaps it was not so hard – in a sense, the blame was not theirs alone. I struggled again and again to let the bitterness go – but it was only after I met the King that I found I could'.

'Why? What difference did that make?' he asked almost angrily.

'He forgave me', she said in a low voice. 'So how could I go on refusing to forgive?'

'If only I had met him too, Kerry!' he said brokenly. 'My heart sometimes almost bursts with bitterness – I hate the very thought of my mother!'

'You will, you will meet him', she assured him earnestly, 'and he will set you free too! Please take comfort, dear Ivan – I feel quite certain that you will have his help in whatever lies ahead'. He did not reply, but she saw that the tense look was eased; and both were aware that it had been good to share, at last, their inner pain.

For a long time they sailed on in silence, busy with their own thoughts. Kerry learned to paddle the coracle, and felt a sense of peace, almost a dreamlike quality, as the craft cut noiselessly through the water. She felt she could have gone on in this peaceful way forever. It was a long time later that she realised Ivan was looking anxiously at the sky. It had turned ominously black; she saw that the birds no longer called in the joy of the spring day, but wheeled and circled with the restlessness of those who saw with secret eyes. The air was oppressively close. Ivan caught her gaze and said: 'A storm is brewing, Kerry'. He said nothing more. Again the stillness was broken only by the sound of endless drops of water as they ran from the lifted oar. They exchanged places. Kerry, watching the land, saw the first crimson tongue of lightning as it flickered above the northern sky: when it came again it was nearer, like a crimson flare; and as it vanished, the first great peal of thunder rolled amid the heavens. And now the sky became as a battlefield of giants; chains of argent clouds were illumined by a hundred tongues of lightning, and as they struck the peaks, every outline was for a moment brightly lit. The scene was both starkly beautiful and awe-inspiring, and the girl found herself shivering.

Then the lightning was closer again, stabbing the darkness in vivid forks like the tongues of dragons: when it came next, it seemed as if the silhouettes of a million trees were painted clearly before her eyes. The pines – how she loved them! Forever they would remain close to her heart, never to be forgotten as the silent witnesses of her meeting with the King – the night of her healing. She wondered if the storm would pass quickly; then immediately she seemed to become aware that it would not, because it was part of the Voice's evil design, the onward march of his relentless crushing of Pyrus. Suddenly, as she looked towards the forest, she saw one pine which had been set on fire by the lightning blazing fiercely; then she found herself weeping, like a mother for her children, as the fire ran on among the pines in a conflagration none could quench.

'Look, Ivan!' she cried out in anguish – 'the Woods of Fall!' Then she was stabbed by the recollection of Falliope and his people – surely they were in grave danger now? Her thoughts went to them with such intensity that she could not have told whether or not she imagined it; she was running, running through the forest ahead of the flames, shouting with all her strength, crying to the people to flee. She felt the fire with dreadful power racing after her, the greedy flames engulfing everything which stood in their way. She became aware that Ivan was crying out: 'The fawns, Kerry! It will destroy the fawns!' in a voice of pure agony. He was weeping too, both of them caught in the pain of helplessness, powerless against the onslaught of the cruel Voice. Another part of Pyrus was doomed, and they were condemned to watch, unable to stop the outrage.

It seemed to Kerry that for many hours the fire raged, while the coracle took them steadily towards the western land. At last the storm was passing; the last of the lightning flashed above the southern Strells. It was almost dark when Kerry felt the coracle slide upon a ledge of rock and touch the gravel of an island shore. Still dazed with pain through all that they had witnessed, they stumbled out of the craft on to the shingled shore. They found a sheltered place under an overhanging bank where they lay down to rest, more exhausted by emotional suffering than they had been earlier by the toil of long journeys through snow and ice. And while they slept, the first soft rain was falling gently upon the broken land, and the last crimson flames of the greedy fire burned, satiated at last; and where the beautiful ranks of pines had stood, there was only blackness and emptiness.

Chapter 5

Pyrus

In the silence of the new day, the travellers ate briefly of the remaining provisions given them by Falliope, while the green land around them was drenched in the rain which had been falling for hours. The fire and storm of the day before still haunted their very souls; they remained with them like the pale ghosts of nightmares long gone, or like childhood fears now come true. They spoke little; in the heart of each was the pain of having as it were witnessed the wrenching out of the very core of the land of Pyrus. Their dreams had been filled with terrifying visions of fire – for Kerry, a fire which became at times the inflamed eyes of the Priests, as they had scorched her on the day Peter was killed. She tried desperately to recapture in her tortured mind a picture of the King's face in its radiance and peace, but even that was for the moment quite gone from her mind.

Without a word they climbed back into the coracle. Gone now was the happy excitement of the day before when they had found it. Yet as they set off towards the western shore, a kingfisher darted nearby, and larks soared in the sky above. A measure of comfort returned unbidden to their bleak spirits. They could not at first bring themselves to look up at the slopes behind, where the forest had been, fearing to see the land charred and bitter under the last of the smoke; then, as the girl was about to take over the oar, she allowed her eyes to travel over the high ground stretching to the far horizon. 'Oh, Ivan, look!' she cried suddenly as relief flooded her heart, 'the forest is not all burned! The river must have halted the fire!' The boy quickly surveyed the far hillside. Despite the rocking of the craft, they embraced each other while tears of joy and relief poured down Kerry's cheeks. Without doubt, the River Elidon – her beloved river – had saved one side of the pine forest; the Voice was not yet victor!

Now they gazed keenly, noting the extent of the destruction. This time it was Ivan who shouted to the girl to look: 'The fawns, Kerry! Look, far up on the hillside, as far as you can see, surely that is a line of deer moving down towards the lower part of the remaining forest? Can you not see?' At first she could not – she had for long been aware that his eyesight was sharper than her own – but at last she saw them; it was indeed the Fawns, how many it was impossible to tell at such a distance; they must have crossed the river high up and now were making their way down into the deeper part of what was left of the Woods of Fall.

'Some may well have perished', Ivan said in a low voice, 'but how good to know that at least a remnant is left! And indeed there may be more within the forest', he added. For a time they could only sit, saying nothing, glad and thankful despite the sadness and hurt of all they had suffered. 'As for the people', said the boy at last, 'let us try to reach Pyrus as soon as we can, so that we may find out whether the Eternal Flame still burns. At least we can now hope; if the Fawns, or some of them, survived, surely there is a chance that they too still live?'

From then on there was but a single desire in both their minds – to find the ruins of the sacked city. They soon reached the farthest edge of the Reed Lands and left the ancient coracle which had served them so well. Now they turned northwards, the words of Falliope still clear and strong in the boy's mind, instructing him to turn north from the western rim of the Reed Lands, and from there behold the low peak beneath whose slopes the ruined city lay. Yet at these times Ivan always felt, with deep unease, that his inner sense already knew which way to turn; then he would recall the ominous words of the Priest: 'Surely you must know that it was the Voice who led you, that he might one day play with you in his domain?' The cold hand of fear would grip his heart. Was it true? Did the evil being still have a hold upon their minds? To Kerry he said nothing; she had enough fears of her own.

For a long time they went on with few words spoken. Above

them stretched, seemingly endlessly, a rock-strewn hill. They reached at last a ridge which fell in slopes of scree to a great bowl. Looking down, they saw with a mixture of excitement and apprehension that in the middle of the bowl could be discerned the blackened ruins of houses. All around them there seemed to be nothing but a deadly silence, the everlasting silence of a devastated land which had been laid waste by the malign might of the Voice.

Hand in hand, slipping on the scree, they began without a word to descend towards the valley. They saw below them a lake which seemed to lie on the outskirts of the ruined city. With foreboding now uppermost in their minds, their feet at times buried deeply in the scree, they finally reached the char-red remains of a street. Kerry felt now as if she had truly arrived at the domain of the Voice – she held fast to Ivan's hand as together they passed through the remains of a stone archway, the ancient gate of Pyrus. Unspeaking, fearing to break the silence of that place of desolation, they walked the streets of the once-proud city, seeing the carved stones with images of days long gone – of warriors, of ships, of animals and birds, of ordinary people at their daily work. The walls loomed like ghosts before them; they found the hollow shells of temples, of palaces, of citadels, where bats now hung silent in the shadows. Darkness was falling fast; the moon was now visible. A bell swung high above the cobbled street, and as the breeze caught it, its single note seemed to toll the knell of the great city like a dire warning to the valley, a warning which nobody now could hear. An archway loomed beside them in the shadows, a low entrance to ruined walls, above whose lintel, deeply carved, could be seen outlined the form of an owl. But even the owl made no sound.

When at last Ivan spoke, the sadness in his voice was almost tangible. 'We must see what this building was, Kerry,' he whispered, 'see what they built in honour of your King.' And as she looked questioningly at him, he nodded as if to quell her doubt. 'Yes, I know in my heart it was for him! In the strangest way, which I cannot possibly explain, I have felt his nearness in this place, and especially here – I am certain this was a shrine. Oh, Kerry, forgive me that I ever doubted, even mocked you. I know now that I want him to be my King too! He is our only comfort, our only source of hope.' In spite of all the desolation, desolation around her and in her spirit, Kerry's heart leapt with joy. The King – she found she could see his face again – would be Ivan's King as well! One day, when the time of sadness was past, they would see him again together. Courage returned to her.

She walked behind her companion beneath the dark archway, the owl above watching unblinkingly, into the courtyard lit up by the moonlight. Tall pillars rose up around them, forming an inner sanctuary paved with huge stones and strewn with pieces of pillars which had been broken. They knew now that they had reached the ancient heart of Pyrus, and were eager to search out its secret. In the very centre stood a beautiful carved image, a statue of a boy child and a girl child; their hands were joined and held above them, almost it seemed as if in defiance of the signs of carnage and destruction all around – everywhere the eye turned could be clearly seen the charred bones of the proud inhabitants of the ancient city. Kerry cried out in horror to see that place so cruelly profaned; Ivan quickly led her away from the chamber, out again into the silver night, into the empty street with its memories of lost grandeur.

'It is true, is it not,' Ivan said, 'they built that place in honour of your King – *our* King?' She could hear the anger in his words, yet her heart lifted again because she knew he had accepted her King as his. 'They built it to show their love,' he continued in a low voice, 'and those evil ones killed them in the very place of peace. The Woods of Fall and Pyrus, all destroyed at the pleasure of the Voice!' Suddenly he burst out in anguish: 'All these have been lost, and I can bear that – but how could I ever bear to lose you, Kerry?'

'Do not despair, dear Ivan,' she answered softly, burying her head in his shoulder, 'remember there is still love, even after death – he said so! Share your sadness with him, with the King. Let him grieve for what is lost, for he first made it.'

She was striving to recall the words of the King, desperate to share them with him just as she had heard them spoken; she must let him understand something of that light which had been shown her, of the new hope and strength she had been given. All the time the ancient bell tolled faintly above them, mournful in the night breeze. She looked up at her companion and he seemed lost in thought; she wondered if he had even heard her urgent words.

Now it was she who led him on, along the moonlit avenue, a path of pure silver leading towards the lake. She looked at Ivan again; the sadness in his face stabbed her heart. At least, she thought, we must find some place of shelter to rest – perhaps a building on the outskirts which had escaped destruction? On they walked in silence for a while; then, unbelievably, Kerry saw a faint light in the distance. At first she said nothing – surely she must be mistaken? Nothing moved in this place of dereliction! But it *was* a light, a tiny, flickering gleam like that of a candle. 'Ivan', she aroused him from his reverie, 'can that possibly be a light?' He looked up, startled, and saw it. 'Someone still lives here, Kerry', he breathed in wonder.

'Not the Priests?' she asked in sudden fear.

Quietly they approached, seeing that the light came from a small, half-ruined cottage. Timidly they knocked and waited, while someone inside came to the door. An old man dressed in rags stood there, looking at them as if he dared not believe what he saw. 'Ah, strangers, welcome!' he cried in a hoarse voice, 'whoever you are, you cannot know how welcome is the sight of living people to a lonely heart like mine! Come in and share what we have, though indeed it is not much'. An old woman was bent over the feeble flame of a fire; she straightened slowly, looking at the travellers in disbelief. 'Forgive us, friends', the old man quavered, 'we have forgotten how to greet strangers! But stay with us, and it may be the old ways of courtesy will return to us'. At this the woman came shyly towards them and gave a withered hand first to Kerry and then to Ivan. 'Food', she whispered, 'what we have . . . welcome'. It was almost as if speech had become a forgotten art with her. She busied herself in setting out a frugal repast, while the old man explained that they had only the meagre food they were able to grow themselves. While the travellers ate, he plied them with questions – where had they come from? Had they seen the Priests? For a long time Ivan and Kerry spoke: they told of the caves, of the death of Peter, of the encounter with the

Priests. 'Ah, the evil ones', breathed the old man. 'They came here and laid waste our beautiful city! But go on with your story first, my friend, and then I shall tell you of our own sufferings'. Ivan now spoke of Falliope and his people in their forest home; the man, whose name was Trirem, at once interrupted: 'And the Woods of Fall? Did you see the graceful guardians of our race?' At the tidings of the fire, tears ran down the wasted cheeks; the old woman too came close to hear every word of the sad story. Then Ivan told of the horn of Celroc and the White Fawn.

'He is the Fawnleader!' Kerry could not help bursting out, 'and he found the dark crystal of the White Fawn!'

The sad old faces were transformed. 'The Fawnleader!' they cried in joy as one. 'You are the one foretold by Celroc, the one whose coming would save our people!', Trirem went on, 'alas that so few of them remain to see this day!' For a time they were silent, as if mulling over the astounding news they had just heard; then, recalling his duty as host, the old man piled more wood on the fire and invited them to sit by the blaze and hear the tale of the sack of Pyrus. In horror the two listened, hearing what in part they knew already, of how the Priests came in force, the owls on their shoulders, and set fire to the city and killed its people.

'We watched, the two of us, from the hillside', the man quavered, 'where we had been gathering wood for our fire, and we saw them leave. It was three days before we found the courage to return'. His voice died away. He stared for a long time into the fire, as if re-living the scene of carnage which had met them on their return. Then he went on: 'We found our house still smouldering. This room is all that is left; ever since, we have lived in it just as it is'. He was quiet again; then he added: 'It was a terrible attack, an attack by the cruel ruler we know as the Voice. But I have to say that some of our people had turned to evil ways, forsaking the true beliefs of former days – sometimes I wonder if we were not punished because of these things'. He shook his head mournfully, and again stared into the flames. They sat in silence again until the woman, Elred, suggested that the travellers must surely be weary and she would bring blankets so that they might sleep.

She then brought them each a woollen covering, tattered but clean; and they lay down where they were, grateful for shelter and warmth.

Kerry found comfort in watching the flickering flames, but it seemed many hours before sleep came to her.

Chapter 6

The Eternal Flame

Ivan, awakening refreshed at first light, knew without hesitation what he must do. It was still very early; the fire still showed some life. He looked across at the sleeping old couple, then, with a look of tenderness, at Kerry who lay near him, the dark circles still visible beneath her eyes. Yes, it was right that she should sleep; he would go alone to find the Eternal Flame. Silently he went out.

Remembering again with absolute clarity the detailed directions given him by Falliope, he did not hesitate but took the road which led to the lake. He drank of its cool water and felt refreshed; then he splashed more on his face, and went on, finding more refreshment in looking around at the hills which circled the ancient site. It was a few moments before the grim memory of the revelations of the night before returned, and he found himself shivering as the full horror came back to his mind. Leaving the shore, he easily saw the long ledge of rock within which, he knew, a gallery of stone was carved into deep caves; resolutely he left the sunlight behind and walked into the shadow. At first darkness seemed to engulf him; the memory of the caves which had swallowed his childhood struck him with almost physical force; nausea and claustrophobic fear threatened to overcome him. Then he seemed to hear Maria's voice, reminding him that what he did was for them all – for the Unborn, his own people. How many times since he left her, he reflected, had he had to keep going forward when everything within him bade him turn back! And so it would be, until at length he met the Voice himself. A wave of nausea and pure fear rose in him again, but he went on, finding soon that his eyes were becoming used to the darkness.

As he reached the first great gallery of stone, he could see that bubbles of lava had burst and then cooled in strange, twisted shapes; the effect was eerie, and added fuel to his apprehension. Quietly he walked on, hearing nothing but the sound as of a river rushing far below. Then he found himself descending fast, under the ruined city, to find at last a honeycomb of caves. Soon he was in a low passage, a place in which he was forced to crouch; beyond, he glimpsed the greyness of light ahead. And when he left the low way, he stood upon a ledge that jutted out from the walls of the tunnel, and saw that a huge cavern stretched before him. Far below a river plunged, foaming and frothing in its steep descent. He called aloud, and the echoes of his call rolled back, over and over, adding to the eeriness of that strange and lonely place.

He left the cavern then and went on through passage after passage, until he came at last to another great cavern with a roof that arched high above. And then as his eyes began to focus more clearly, he beheld a glow, a light that shone in the very heart of the huge cave. His heart leapt; he knew beyond all doubt that the object of his quest was here. The Flame still burned! Then surely Falliope and some of his people still lived! Swiftly he moved forward towards the small corona of flame that shone clear in the darkness of the place. It was indeed a feeble flame, yet not so nearly extinguished as might indicate only the survival of Trirem and Elred; no, he felt an assurance in his heart that a goodly number of the Pyrians must yet be alive. How good it would be to tell Kerry! Yet, even as his heart lifted at this thought, there swept over him again the enormity of the destruction and death he and Kerry had witnessed, and despair came upon him. He gave a groan of pure misery.

'Do you despair, Fawnleader?' The startling words came at him suddenly from the darkness behind. He turned quickly, and saw a form silhouetted in the archway of the cavern. The figure advanced slowly towards him, the footsteps echoing dully upon the stone floor, the robe that enveloped his person becoming clearer as he moved towards the dim flame. Then he was standing beside him, beside the bowl holding the Flame, his hands clasped about it as though he would have extinguished it for ever. Ivan stood still, holding his hands clenched together to stop their trembling: he saw that there was no owl on the Priest's shoulder, nor did anyone accompany him into the cave. They two were alone. Turning at last to look at his face, Ivan recoiled at the sight of the burning eyes which seemed like two coals drawn from the surface of the sun – they glowed with pure evil. Suddenly the dreaded face was near his own, leering cruelly, and hands were around his neck, horribly constricting his throat. He was forced to his knees.

'Do you wonder to see me here?', he snarled, 'you whom they call the Fawnleader, and do you perhaps wonder why I am alone and without the symbol of his power? Ah, then I shall tell you, before you hand over the crystal and before I kill you, slowly, and you are burned up in the last vestiges of the flame!' He laughed horribly, the sound echoing through the cavern, and Ivan felt his fetid breath as his face pressed close to his own. His throat burned as fingers like the talons of eagles pressed into his flesh; his whole body felt drained of strength.

He heard the rasping voice go on: 'I am Leon, the last to be made a Priest, but first to see the burning of Pyrus; and first too to desecrate the Temple of their King! But when I touched the statue, the symbol of creation formed of the first rocks of the earth, then the Voice could hold me no longer, and I was free! Free, I tell you – free to practise my own evil instead of his!' The words rang out in the cavern with malicious glee. 'The owl on my shoulder returned to him', he continued, 'returned to alert him that I was no longer under his command; but I am free to seek the revenge I have desired ever since he first enslaved me. And now you, Fawnleader' – again the terrible laugh rang out in mockery – 'you will hand over the gem, and I shall become master of Pyrus. And there will be nobody, nobody, I tell you, to rob me of the kingdom which shall be mine!'

Ivan felt himself drowning in a sea of pain. His eyes danced with crimson lights as the blood surged and his throat was crushed agonisingly. 'Give me the stone!' hissed the Priest in his ear; 'I have waited long enough!' But he could not, would not: it was his people's only hope. Better surely to die than hand it over, to fail them now. And then he heard himself give a strangled cry, which echoed over and over in the darkness.

Still the terrible face leered above him, a face of madness and wickedness beyond imagining; and then he felt as if he were falling as if the very ground had opened beneath him, as if darkness and emptiness waited to swallow him. Yet from somewhere deep within there came the tiniest flicker, a small gleam of courage; and struggling to hold on to it, he summoned up his failing strength and forced himself to face the Priest again.

With all that was left of his voice he shouted as loudly as he could: 'No, Leon, no, no, no! Yours was never the destiny to conquer him!' So startled that he loosed his grip of Ivan's throat, the Priest screamed in fury, glaring at him with his burning malevolent eyes.

'You lie. Fool and liar! Nobody shall rob me of my destiny! The kingdom will be mine!' Turning, he beat his hands in frenzy on the rock on which the Flame burned.

Again the flicker of courage returned, and the boy went on: 'No, no, you are wrong! One thing I do know – it is not you who are destined to find the stone and make it whole again!' The Priest gave a great roar of fury and frustration; again he turned away and beat the rock with his hands. Seizing his chance, Ivan lunged at him with every last vestige of his strength: with another roar of rage the Priest fell awkwardly sideways, his hand in the Flame. Howling with pain he fell backwards, his head striking a rock.

For one fleeting moment the boy watched him, spent; then he turned and ran from the cavern. Slipping, stumbling, the blood pounding in his ears, he forced himself on through passage after passage, cave after cave; his throat ached with a pain such as he had never felt before, but not once did he slacken his pace. At last, half-swooning, he found to his infinite relief that there was daylight ahead. Somehow, it seemed a long time after, he reached the shores of the mere; a drink from the refreshing waters revived him, and for a time he bathed his throbbing throat. Then slowly he began to make his way back to Trirem's house. Soon he saw a familiar figure coming towards him. He tried to call out to Kerry but the effort was too great; soon they were sitting in the sun, while she heard his story and comforted him. He lay beside her, soothed by her nearness, and in a few moments was asleep.

It was only a short time, but he awoke rested and calmed. He found Kerry watching him anxiously. 'What is wrong?' he asked, noting her concern.

'Ivan, I am so afraid that he will come – that the Priest, Leon, will pursue us!', she blurted out. 'He must surely know that you have the stone?'

'Perhaps you are right', agreed the boy. 'But do not be afraid – I know it will not be soon. He is injured – how badly I do not know; but I feel sure he will not yet be fit to follow us'. He was quiet for a moment, and then said: 'Forgive me, Kerry; there was no other way'. She looked at him, uncomprehending, and he explained: 'I hated to use such violent means to get rid of him! You are gentleness itself; I dreaded even to tell you of it. And the King . . .', he tailed off.

'Please, please, Ivan', she replied earnestly, 'do not think I cannot understand! Everything you do is for others as well as ourselves – there was no choice; he would certainly have killed you!'

She went on to tell him how she had awakened to find him gone, and had known at once where he must be. 'I explained to Trirem and Elred what you had to do', she told him, 'and then, when we had eaten, I helped them work on their little plot of land. But they need wood for their fire, Ivan; and it is hard for them to carry heavy loads. Could we gather some for them before we go?' The boy at once agreed, and they went together to the cottage. Ivan told the story of his time in the caves while he ate what had been kept for him; the old couple applauded with eyes that seemed to have regained some of the sparkle of youth. Then, with gratitude, they accepted the offer of help in gathering a store of fuel.

As Ivan and Kerry worked, they talked. It had seemed to the boy that they would be well advised to stay another night in the ruined city. 'No, Ivan', said Kerry quietly, 'This is to be the day – the day when I go to meet the shadow'.

At first he could not take in the awful words which she spoke so calmly. He stopped and sat down, while the world seemed to spin around him, and a tight band of pain made him feel as if his heart would stop. He looked at her face, pale but serene.

Then at last he managed quietly: 'Tell me, Kerry'. She sat beside him and held his hand tightly.

'Last night was bad, Ivan', she said. 'I mean, my dreams – they have been getting worse . . . the approach of the shadow, as I told you before, and the black wings blocking out the light'. She shuddered and then went on resolutely. 'You remember the other day, when I wept and told you I was losing the light?'

'But now you are so calm!' he said wonderingly. 'Oh Kerry, what your secret is I do not know – but please, do not expect me to share it! I cannot bear to lose you, and nothing can ever change that!'

She held his hands more tightly, and then continued: 'After that time when I came close to panic, it seemed as if I could only remember the whispers of the Voice – I thought I would go mad if I could find no way of standing against the evil. And then I saw what I should have seen long ago, Ivan – there was indeed a way! As the Voice is the essence of evil, so is the King the essence of good! So I made a resolve that every time I felt the approach of the shadow, I would remember the King's face, and keep it in my mind with all my might; and I would recall his words, and say them over and over until calmness had returned'.

'And did you succeed?', he asked her, now inexplicably calmed himself.

'Not all the time', she answered truthfully, 'but the oftener I tried, the more strength I seemed to receive'.

Again she lapsed into silence, and the boy, fighting for mastery over his emotions, watched her with a mixture of deep sadness and overwhelming love. 'And then this morning, after you had gone, he came to me – suddenly the King was there! Perhaps in a dream, perhaps not; I cannot be sure. But he spoke to me, and told me I would always belong to him' – her voice faltered for a moment – 'and you too, Ivan! He said you are one whose heart belongs to him'. Ivan, choked with emotion, could not speak. 'And then he told me I must listen carefully, and remember everything he said. This is what it was: "Never give way to evil; I am the one who overcomes evil. Never believe the lies of the Voice; I am the truth. Strive not to fear death; love is stronger than death. And above all, remember that death is not the end". That is all, Ivan'.

For a long moment he held her close, feeling that his heart must break for love of her. With a great effort he then asked her to repeat the words, and resolutely spoke them after her. In silence they rose and went on with building a store of fuel for their hosts.

Despite the morning which had passed, it was still not long past noon when they said a sad farewell to Trirem and Elred. Although the old couple would fain have had them stay, they yet realised the urgent necessity for their going: they gave them their blessing with tears in their eyes, the words of the old man unconsciously echoing those of Maria as he said: 'What you do is for us all – for your race, the Unborn, and for us, the people of Pyrus. Farewell, young friends, and may you come safely to your journey's end! You shall have our gratitude forever!'

The young pair did not look back as they left behind the lonely old man and woman in the ruins of their home. At first Kerry walked a little in front, and in silence they went on, listening to the larks above them in the clear sky, hearing the laughing streams, absorbing the scents of the green countryside; all the beauty of their surroundings seemed to Ivan merely to accentuate the deep sorrow which welled up in his heart. Then Kerry stopped and waited for him, and said to his surprise, 'Ivan, I want to sing for you'. He looked so bewildered that she went on: 'Oh, I know none of us ever sang in the caves – there was no reason to sing there. But when you were away climbing Mount Gilrene, after I was healed, Falliope's people taught me to sing! I found learning easy, Ivan – and today I want to sing you the song they taught me'. She did not say, because it will be the last time, but they both knew the reason; he felt he would not be able to bear it, and yet, longing to hear her voice, he managed to say: 'Dearest Kerry, sing it to me'.

She began to sing, and in the beauty of the melody and the sweetness of her voice it seemed to him that the sorrow in his soul grew less, and the darkness was for the moment lightened. Her lovely face was now illumined by the radiance of her pure spirit; and although her eyes were dark-rimmed with grief, a light still shone in them, triumphing over the doom which lay ahead. Evil would never conquer her.

'I have walked where mere meets sky
The plains like argent beaten sheets
Of steel beneath the sun.

'I have heard the skylarks singing
Calling for their darkened homeland
Far above the shattered earth.

'I have drunk from streams untarnished
Plunging from the towering ice-crests
Rainbowed in the golden light.

'I have laughed with doves from heaven
Circling in the azure brightness
Carrying the seeds of peace'.

He could not speak; he held her close, and her head was on his shoulder as they went on, walking more slowly now, listening to the song of the larks which seemed to fill the sky above them.

Suddenly the girl's control broke: 'Oh Ivan', she cried brokenly, 'I am so afraid – and I cannot see the King's face any more!' He sought to comfort her as best he could, for his own heart felt as heavy as lead.

'But you have not lost him', he assured her. 'Did he not promise to stay with you always?'

'I know you are right; I know he has not really gone – it's just that I'm afraid – afraid of the darkness! And Ivan, I am so ashamed; how can I be so faithless, when just this morning he was there – he came to me!'

Ivan was silent for a while, and then he said: 'Kerry, my beloved, let us do as you taught me just a little while ago; let us say together the words of the King'. They sat down on a mossy bank, and in quiet voices which gained in assurance as they went on, they began to repeat: 'Never give way to evil; I am the one who overcomes evil. Never believe the lies of the

Voice; I am the truth. Strive not to fear death; love is stronger
than death. Remember that death is not the end'.

She said quietly: 'Thank you, dear Ivan. These things will
always be true, not just for me but also for you in – in whatever
may lie ahead after – after I have left you'. Tears welled in her
eyes, but she went on: 'And we must remember that our sacrifice must be made willingly'. A wave of pure love for her swept
over the boy again, a love deep as oceans, a love that would
never break, even in the final separation. Now for the last time
he held her close, held her as he had so often held her, in a
warm embrace that had been their sanctuary as children, when
they were fearful and lost, unloved and rejected by a world in
which no place had been found for them. They were as one,
bound together by cords of love. So much there had been to
break their spirits – the malice of the Voice amid the cruel life
of the caves, the agony of Peter's death, the bitterness of the
winter cold, the burning of the Woods and of the doomed city.
And yet in this moment, out of their suffering a kind of joy
had been born, and a pure flame of love had been drawn as it
were out of the harshest chill of winter; somehow out of the
utter desolation of the land they both loved, seeds of hope had
come.

'There will be another time, another place,' whispered Kerry,
and her voice was steady despite her tears. 'We shall know one
day that the land is free, free from the malice of the Voice
forever. Do you believe that now, Ivan?' He nodded and smiled,
unable to speak. 'Do not fail', she said. She turned then and
left him, the child he had always loved, the one who had
laughed and played and wept with him, who had known his
heart as nobody else ever would. The sun on her hair touched
it to gold; the wind lifted it. She did not look back, but walked
steadily and with her head held high. He did not follow, for
both knew without a word spoken that she alone must go
forward to meet the shadow.

Chapter 7

The Well

It seemed a long way to the well, the ancient place of which the old man, Trirem, had told her. When at last she saw it, her heart told her unerringly that this was indeed her last walk. How strange it was to her that fresh green grass still grew under her feet, and that the skylarks called joyously in the clear azure sky!

As for Ivan, he watched her go, and his very heart and soul went with her: not for a moment could he take his eyes off the beloved, slender form. Like a special envoy bringing a blessing, a skylark came and trilled his liquid song immediately above her: the boy's eyes filled with tears as she turned at last and pointed upwards as if acknowledging the small miracle. Blinded, he could not see her until she was some distance away; then he watched until her form had shrunk in the distance. He saw her sit down on a rock – no, it must be the well of which Trirem had spoken.

As she sat, he suddenly saw coming swiftly towards her from the empty sky a form which seemed to corrupt the beauty of the day, a shadow whose wings beat like those of a giant moth, whose hoarse cry brought to his heart a chill of ice. A white owl - one of the Priests' evil companions! He saw it rush at her, attacking her again and again; and already, freed as it were from the restraints placed upon him, he was running, running madly with all the strength he possessed, running to save his dear love too precious to lose. All his former acceptance of her death now forgotten, he ran on while groans of sheer agony broke from him. He saw nothing in these moments, merely was aware of the harsh cries of the attacker. Then he was at the well, and in utter disbelief and despair he realised that she had gone – she was nowhere to be seen. With raucous cries the bird of ill repute was now some distance away.

'Kerry! Kerry!' he called out in agony of spirit; his cry filled the darkness of the yawning pit, at the bottom of which he now, in unbelieving horror, saw spreadeagled in pathetic frailty his beloved companion. She was dead – there could be no possible doubt. The Voice had struck the cruellest blow of all. That which he had most greatly feared had come to pass at last.

Madness for the moment almost overwhelmed him. He raised his fists against the now empty skies, crying out uselessly: 'Was there not enough blood in Pyrus to satisfy your lust?' But he heard nothing – there was nothing, only the ragged tatters of the wind that beat about his ravaged, empty heart. He would hear her voice for ever, that sweet voice that had sung so short a time ago, the voice of one who had known how to love with all her heart. When no memories remained, he thought bitterly, and the despair of her passing had settled on his soul, still he would hear her song. He sank down on the mossy ground by the well and wept as if his spirit had been shattered for ever.

Then he seemed to hear her voice saying, saying along with his own voice that very morning: 'Strive not to fear death; love is stronger than death. Remember that death is not the end'. What did it really mean? Was it true, could it possibly be true, that death was not the end? But surely it must be true, for the King was very truth. Then he would see her again! He must hold on to that hope; had she not also said: 'These things will always be true – in whatever may lie ahead after I have left you'. He must not fail her by not believing them as she did. And her last words had been: 'Do not fail'. He must not fail – not her, and not the Unborn. Once again, although everything in him cried out to give up the struggle and turn back, he must go on; indeed, how could he possibly go back? Where would he go? As he reasoned all these things, slowly a measure of comfort began to steal into his sad and wounded heart. Once more he forced himself to look down into the well, the place of horror; then he knew beyond all doubt that this was not his Kerry – she was no longer there.

And so at last he turned from darkness to light, from death to life. And it seemed almost as if her soul, the very essence of her being, came to be with him then, running like a child upon the green grassland, laughing in the sweetness of the spring air; and sometimes in his imagination she turned to him and smiled, for a fleeting moment before she faded and was gone.

He began to walk faster then as if with her spirit for companion, with a Kerry who now wept no more, for whom the pain and fear were gone, and it seemed to him that it was she who gave him the courage to face at last the shadow of the twin peaks and the dreaded Underland which now lay before him. Mighty and dark these high pillars soared, menacing, above the sunlit plains, mountains which he already felt to be tainted with the malignant breath of the Voice. Once, he knew, a pine-covered valley had lain between the rocky slopes of Fer-Elen and Moravadel, the twins; now its heart was blackened too by the fire's desolation, and by a mist that wreathed thickly in its rocky pass, hiding all else behind. And the mountainside, once said to have been resplendent in an array of blossoms of a hundred hues, was dying now under the weight of vast, skull-like boulders which had fallen from the heights above, lying beneath the mist-filled valley that had lost the blessing of the sun.

He saw that pass of death far to the north, the very heart of the domain of the Voice, where even now his doomed servants toiled. Was Kerry going to them, he wondered with a terrible lurch of the heart? Was she even now on her way to join the people she loved, over the sunlit plain to the land of darkness? He could not bear it. Now he felt that her spirit had left him. 'Kerry!' he called in a voice which came out in an agonised groan. 'Kerry, come back!' But there was nothing, nothing but the sound of the breeze, and nobody listened to his weeping. Once his heart leapt as he fancied she turned to him again and smiled; but then again she was gone, and though he should cry for her to the end of time, she would not return to him.

And so wearily, he trod the plains alone. At last, before the sunlight finally gave way to the darkness, he reached the last plain under the shadow of the peaks: the Underland was now before him, and he found in his heart a mixture of excitement and fear. He wished now only to press on, to find the land that lay below all light, to face the trial which had so often blotted out the light for him. A little below him, he could see the outline of a lake; his spirit lifted a little at the sight of it – he would go and drink, and bathe his tired feet. When he reached it, he walked into the cool water until his feet were covered; then, on impulse, he found himself kneeling in the water, and felt a strange sense of solace in that moment. 'Fawnleader!' The word was spoken so softly that for a moment he wondered if he had dreamed it. He turned curiously and looked all around, but there was nothing, nothing save the faint sound of the waves on the shore. Then the call came again. 'Fawnleader! It is I, the one Kerry met in the Woods of Fall, when she was healed! You doubted me at first – how hard for you to understand! The stain of darkness and sorrow has been left upon your heart, yet it will not be long until you are washed in the pure fountain made ready for you, my servant who did not fail!'

The voice was balm to his weary, troubled soul. He looked up, and although he did not see the form of the King, he seemed to glimpse as it might be his shadow upon the waters of the mere; and he was aware of his nearness. Tears of joy flowed. He knelt again in the cool water, this time with a sense of deep gratitude; and all at once he found himself speaking to the King, the true King of Pyrus, the one who had given the lark its voice, whose hand had set the stars in their courses, whose word of command had brought the farthest seas into being. How strange and wonderful it seemed!

'I feel old with trouble and sorrow, my Lord', he said. 'You granted healing and new life to Kerry: I pray you will grant new life and healing of spirit to me, for I am in great need'.

'My son', he heard the King's voice reply gently, 'you have been more obedient to your destiny than all who have gone before you, all the souls who strove but did not have your strong endurance. And you have tried to carry on your shoulders a burden too great for you, one which only I can bear. Know that I understand your weariness'.

For a few moments Ivan heard nothing, and he feared lest the King had gone; then he heard him speak again. 'But you will have strength for the end of your path. The place of death and destruction will be the place where you will finally realise your power! You will both conquer and be conquered, vanquish and be vanquished, for that is what I have written, and none may change it. And do not doubt, my son – the dark crystal of which you hold a part will indeed be made whole, whose other part is hidden in the depths of the enemy's domain. Hear and remember my words, Fawnleader – you shall not fail! With Kerry you will find the golden land she saw in dreams, a land more beautiful than words can ever tell. You shall save the Unborn, your own people, and save the land of Pyrus too from final desolation'.

Then there was silence, and this time the boy knew that the King had gone: he heard only the wavelets on the shingled shore. As he thought of all that he had heard, his heart was greatly comforted – how well he could understand now how Kerry had been so changed by meeting him! He thought of how he had first seen her again after she had been healed; how he had said to her, seeing the radiance in her face, 'you look like a new person!' Now he knew that she had indeed been made new; and although at times the darkness had threatened to overcome her, the light had never been put out. And he, Ivan, although he had not himself seen the King, he had heard his voice. If only he could somehow carry the remembrance of this into that place of fear and horror to which he was going! Then his courage would not fail.

He set his face towards the two great peaks, Fer-Elen and Moravadel; these, he knew well, formed the very jaws of the kingdom of the Voice. There, some time later, where the shadows of the peaks joined, his tiny form passed into the dark valley where no sun or warmth ever reached. Knowing there could be no return, he looked back for an instant to glimpse once more the sky of Pyrus, home of the tall pines, the rushing streams, the soaring larks; in his heart he said farewell. Stumblingly, his heart like lead, he went on to be swallowed up in the darkness that lay beyond.

Chapter 8

Descent

Only the croak of ravens could be heard, as they wheeled far above the rock-strewn land; their hoarse cries added to the foreboding of the lonely traveller. Then all at once a new and stranger sound assailed his ears; as the noise increased, he was able to see in the semi-darkness a flock of ram-fowl which came nearer and nearer until they were flying around his head. He shrank away, terrified, seeing their eyes like crimson fire, hearing their unearthly shrieks; their batlike wings gave them an evil mien, and their rank smell nauseated him. When they moved on into the dark region ahead, Ivan, his strength sapped by the encounter, sat down on a rock to regain his composure. He brought out the small satchel containing the last of the bread given him by the old couple in Pyrus, knowing that he would not eat again, and fully aware that the last lap of his journey had truly begun.

With a lurch of his heart he saw below him the dark mouth of a cave; he recognised at once that this was the entrance to the place of second death, the portal through which so many of his people, the Unborn, must have passed on the way to their doom. He who was not yet dead must follow them, to face whatever lay ahead in that grim place. He found that his limbs were trembling. How could he bring himself to face the ultimate horror? How could he even find the courage to rise at this moment and walk towards that yawning, menacing cave mouth? He felt he had lost all power: there was nobody, nobody, to help him. He shut his eyes, and dropped his head on to his folded arms, engulfed for the moment in darkness. Then he seemed to see a tiny pinpoint of light, which grew

until it filled the whole of his vision. He found himself saying
the simple words: 'Help me, my King; I am afraid'.

He stayed in the same position for a moment, seeing and
feeling nothing. Then into his mind came a picture of hands –
first, the misshapen hands of Maria were stretched out towards
him, then the slender hands of Kerry. Kerry! he suddenly felt
her nearness. How short a time since she had been with him,
deeply distressed that she could so soon have known fear,
when the King had come himself to strengthen her. At the
time, he too had wondered why this should be so; now he
could understand. Both he and she were weak, frail creatures;
yet in the end she had so bravely gone to face death, her head
held high! Ah, but she had sought help from the King: he
recalled how they had sat together, their hands clasped, repeating the words of the King. Why should he not do the same now,
although she was no longer with him? Striving to remember the
exact sequence, he began to say aloud: 'Never give way to evil;
I am the one who overcomes evil. Never believe the lies of the
Voice; I am the truth. Strive not to fear death; love is stronger
than death. Above all, remember that death is not the end'. If
the King is the truth, he mused, these words are true. He
must hold to that, even if, as seemed probable, the nearer he
approached to the Voice's domain, the more danger there
would be that his power would over-shadow his mind, even
perhaps take control of his thoughts altogether. He had done
the best he could; now he must go forward in trust.

Greatly comforted, feeling new power flow into his very
limbs, he rose and went towards the sinister aperture. He
walked steadily into its darkness. At once the memory of the
caverns of his childhood rushed at him; yet here, he felt, was
a different kind of darkness, one that was emptiness itself. He
entered the passage, and found that the rugged, rough-hewn
walls echoed as he struck them; as he went farther in, it seemed
to him that they were lit dimly as if by a kind of marshlight.
He perceived with revulsion the faces of demons carved out of
the stone, which leered at him as he passed. He descended into
silent brooding caverns like enormous arched buildings; his
footsteps echoed eerily on the floors of the passages. Stalactites
shimmered high above. He began to hear many weird noises –

at times demented laughter like that of the Priests, at times a
very tumult of murmurings which seemed to echo all around
him. Could these be the clamouring voices of the dead spirits
of the Unborn, crying out for release? The thought filled him
with dread.

In a sudden fearful rushing of sound he found himself in a
dark cavern lit only by a thousand thousand burning eyes. The
cavern, filled with ram-fowl, was to the demented traveller the
final horror; dark wings beat around him, unearthly shrieking
filled the air; their stench revolted him. He turned away, trembling from the onslaught upon his senses, and made his way
to the next chamber. Here a different sight met his gaze – a
huge stalactite hung from the roof, a single white pillar which
reached halfway to the rough stone beneath. On the very tip
of the horn of white hung a clear gem of quivering crystal; the
drop of water then fell into the hollowed rock below. For a time
he was glad to linger, watching the silver drops, hearing them
fall in a rhythm which soothed him as music might have done;
it seemed the only thing to mark the passing of time in that
forgotten subterranean land, the place where darkness reigned.
Then he turned and went on, through passage after passage,
until at length he heard a mighty rushing sound, and found
himself on the banks of a great river which gathered in the
valley above and poured to the heart of the Underland. The
tunnel through which it passed was ending, opening out
beneath him; he walked on the gravel at its side, his eyes
straining to see at last the place he so greatly feared to see, the
place of death. And then he reached the tunnel's mouth, his
ears deafened by the roar of the river as it plunged into the
depths of the earth, his heart grey with foreboding. He struggled on to reach a plateau of piled shingle, and beheld the
kingdom of the dead, a wasteland empty of all that might have
lived, altogether blackened by fire. All was devoid of life.

Standing high, indistinct in the swirling grey mist, was a
gate. He saw at once that it was a thing of great beauty; on it
were carved heads of lordly eagles, and of deer running in
forest glades. It was adorned with beaten gold bars, and he
saw as he came near that some words were carved in the gold;
with a lift of the heart he recognised that they were the words

of the King: 'Let not your head be bowed in grief: the promise
of the dawn is close'. Then the King had once been here! How
could this be, in this place of no hope? Had this once been part
of the kingdom of light? He would not learn the answer to this
mystery here: he must go on. Yet his spirit was cheered.

He reached out then and tried the handle of the gate; to his
surprise, it opened with ease, and he saw the sunless land
stretched out before him, and a cobbled street which he recognised with a sinking heart as the Street of Wailing. How well
he remembered Maria's awesome accounts of this place of no
return, prepared for the dead by the design of the Voice: upon
its rough cobbles there fell a kind of light that formed a path
in front of him, flanked by guardian stones that seemed to
lead away to nothingness. And beyond the farthest stone there
towered a pillar of darkest hue, a finger pointing upward as if
in mockery, evil and silent as the one who waited there in the
darkness of the Underland.

He entered then that land of horror, hearing with fear and
trembling as it were the voices of a thousand thousand unborn
souls who wailed in the utter emptiness and hopelessness of
the Street. Blackness seemed to fill his own soul then and he
wept with them, broken-hearted at their cruel fate, weeping
from the depths of his being as one who was kin to them. They
were the ones without hope, he thought, those who had been
condemned to a life without light or warmth or love, who now
served their vile master without end or reward. They were the
ones who waited for his coming, he thought then with awe,
the ones he dared not fail! Dimly he was aware of weaving
forms which seemed to make way for him: their tears seemed
to be one with his own as he was swept among them. And as
he passed, trembling and afraid, it seemed to him that he began
to hear their voices whispering to him, murmuring as it might
be words of encouragement:

'Fawnleader, be strong; do not fail after coming so far'.

'Ah, we have not waited in vain; even now there is hope for
the Unborn'.

'Welcome, one who lives and yet has come alone to the land
of death. Do not turn back now!'

Their voices reached the depths of his soul; they wounded

him, each one an arrow that pierced his heart. He did not attempt to reply; he knew only that he must on no account fail them, that there would be no other to take his place.

On and on he went, conscious all the time of shadowy forms which at times he fancied bowed to him, as to a king; wailing voices seemed like a wall around him. He lost all track of time as he trod that street of infinite sadness; then far beyond, on the summit of a hill that gleamed dully like a great pile of gathered bones, the sounds changed and he became conscious instead of the evil, mocking laughter he had known all too well as a child, the demented laughter he had learned to associate with the Voice and his Priests. Surely they must be awaiting him there! A chill settled upon his heart. Now he must walk the final bitter way alone, a way no mortal had ever walked before.

He felt all at once as if he carried the wounds of all Pyrus, the wounds of a once beautiful land which lay under the thrall of the evil one he must now face. Yet if he did not offer himself willingly, did not place his very life in the heart of the crystal of life, the dominion of wickedness would not be overcome. His one fear was that the strength within him might not suffice: he knew himself the weakest of all creatures, a mere shadow in this darkest place which had closed its jaws round him, the very frailest who could possibly have been chosen for a mission of such high purpose. He felt frighteningly alone and unprotected. What could have made him imagine for a moment that he stood the slightest chance of overcoming such a mighty foe?

At this lowest point when courage had all but gone, he found himself impelled to look back; he saw that the great gate was now only a faint gleam far behind him. Yet it served to remind him that the King had once been there; and in that moment of utter helplessness his bleak spirit was aware of a small measure of warmth and comfort. Without ever having consciously memorised them, he found himself repeating the King's words engraved on the gate: 'Let not your head be bowed in grief: the promise of the dawn is close'. Suddenly he knew, deep in his being, that even here the King would not fail him; the good, not the evil, would conquer!

Soon a dark doorway loomed before him. Not hesitating now

even momentarily, he grasped the carved door-handle and passed through: as if moved by unseen hands, the door closed behind him. He stood still, hearing an outburst of the familiar mocking laughter. When it ceased, he summoned every shred of courage and shouted at the top of his voice: 'Do you hear me? I have come!' There was no answer, but in a moment another burst of demented laughter rang out, so that he covered his ears with his hands. Silence again. Then he shouted: 'Voice! You have known for long that I would come! Now I am here! I have come to tell you that Pyrus is not conquered – the Flame still burns! And it burns too in my heart, and in the hearts of the Unborn, and above all in the King who will not allow us to fail. There is light still in the darkness!'

There was nothing – no reply, only emptiness. Despite his brave words, Ivan was trembling from head to foot: he felt sick, drained, fearful. He must steady himself before going forward; he would say the words of the King. The words of the King? He could remember nothing – all was blank: it was as he had feared. The Voice was gaining control of his mind! Very well, he thought; there can be no turning back. All I can do is trust that the King will preserve me from failure. And to his great relief he heard within his mind the King's voice as it had whispered to him by the lake: 'You shall not fail!' Once more he took courage and went on.

Now his eyes were straining as he groped his way forward. At last he saw in the far distance a single candle flame. Slowly he stumbled on towards its feeble glow, until beyond it he perceived the beginnings of a low passageway: he had to stoop low to enter the yawning darkness under a rough-hewn roof of rock, and slowly groped farther and farther on until his very soul seemed enclosed, and hopelessness once again rose in him, threatening to overcome his resolve. At last he stumbled and fell forward on his knees. As he looked up, a strange half-light met his gaze, while at the same time his ears were assailed by strange and fearful sounds as of eerie laughter mingled with a kind of resonance coming from the heart of the stone. Half-dazed from weariness and foreboding, he struggled to his feet, and found that he stood upon the very threshold of the dreaded throne-hall, between two carved pillars that shone in the shimmering light, formed of mighty stalactites and stalagmites which had fused together. He had finally come to that place he had both dreaded and longed to reach, where he must either free or forever fail his people.

Chapter 9

The Voice

They had come to stand around him, three tall Priests in flowing robes, and they lashed him with their venomous gaze as others of their number had done before. Trembling from head to foot, Ivan tried to look away; he saw that a fiery torch was set in the very apex of the high-roofed cavern, so bright that it showed clearly every rock, every fissure. Beneath it was a fallen pillar, carved with figures and runic inscriptions. Drawn by the will of another, he was forced to look again into the demonic eyes which seared his soul.

'So you have come at last to serve our master', one of the Priests rasped; an unblinking owl sat on his shoulder.

'Ah, you have had no choice', a second Priest added in a sibilant whisper, his words cold as drawn steel.

'And you shall have no mercy', snarled a third who stood beside the pillar, smiling with malicious triumph. The boy was as if irresistibly drawn to meet each burning gaze; the three Priests moved inexorably closer, forcing him backwards, their faces twisted with rage, until he touched the cold rock behind and could retreat no further. 'Now you will hand over the stone', they seemed almost to spit the words in chorus. Trapped, terrified, Ivan began to believe there was no choice; he felt the gem as it were burning his hand as he clutched it desperately – let him but fling it at their feet, and they would leave him in peace. In peace? But there would be no peace, never any peace again for him, should he fail his people! And all at once he seemed to hear again the voice of the King – Kerry's King, his own King – 'Hear and remember my words, Fawnleader; you shall not fail'. His fearful heart took courage again. This could not be the end. With all his might he shouted 'No!'

Then the Priests drew close around him as he stood under the glare of the brand that burned above, their faces eerie, cruel, greedy in the flickering light, their teeth like the fangs of wolves, their voices babbling insanely: their hands lifted him, set him roughly on the fallen stone pillar on which he saw again the ancient runes carved. And then began a chant which chilled his very soul. Ivan lay still, dazzled by the brilliance of the flame, seeing the faces swim above him, first one and then another, each one more detestable than the last, evil beyond any of the foul nightmares of his childhood. The chanting went on as the Priests slowly circled the stone, until at last he felt he was sinking in a putrid sea, floating as it were on waves of horror and nausea, falling into depths from which he would never again surface. But he did surface; and now the terrible faces were close, so close that the burning eyes seemed to scorch his soul; and the chanting rose and rose about him. They circled the rock on which he lay imprisoned again and again; waves of giddiness swept over him; he tried to shut out the dreadful sound of the chant. He felt his soul sinking into the very darkness of death.

Suddenly he seemed to see before him a land burned and ravaged, an empty world in which nothing of goodness or light or hope remained: then, swimming before his gaze, he saw the pale ghosts of the Unborn, the lost and forgotten ones whom no-one wanted. He fancied he could hear their voices imploring him not to fail them. He fought the blackness then, fought with might and main to return to the light, and as he did so, found that there remained a flicker of warmth inside his fearful heart. He reached upward again and opened his eyes.

The awful chant had ceased. Now the three Priests stood round the slab; crimson flame flickered on their faces; the brand was beginning to burn low. The faces seemed to be sneering at him with a look of evil triumph. Again he felt as if the gem would burn his hand. Suddenly, so clearly that it might have been whispered in his ear, the thought came to him that somewhere in this chamber, the inner domain of the Voice, must be found the other half of the jewel; whatever happened to him, he must to the very last be on his guard, watchful for the opportunity to place the two parts together. Nothing else mattered. Long ago he had made up his mind, freely chosen to offer up his own life that his people might be freed. At this moment he felt certain that the time was fast approaching when this decision would become a reality; he was trapped, encircled by the watching, waiting Priests; they were motionless, clearly waiting – but for whom?

Then he knew. The blood froze in his veins as he heard another voice, one he knew from childhood dreams, and feared above all else; it was like the hiss of a serpent, the utter personification of all he had ever hated, very evil itself come to make an end of him forever. Now the Priests were no longer triumphant: they were servile, kneeling, reduced to the grovelling slaves they were, and the Voice was addressing him, as he lay before him, completely at his mercy. 'Ah, so you have come, creature, the one they call the Fawnleader'. This was the Voice indeed, his enemy for ever. He was darkness, he was emptiness, he was all the horror of death everlasting; he was the foul disease that corrupts the beauty of life, the pain of the brokenhearted, the violence and anger and bitterness of man to man, the bringer of famine and war; he was the murderer and plunderer and destroyer. He was, too, the one who frayed the edges between life and death. In the half-light shed by the now dying brand Ivan saw that he was slowly coming nearer. At last he was beside the slab on which his victim lay.

'I have spared you thus far because it was my will that you should yourself come to my domain to be destroyed', the terrible voice spat the words. 'You thought, fool, that it was through your own strength that you endured'. Now he was bending over Ivan, his burning eyes seeming to search his soul. 'Know this one thing, Fawnleader' – the word was said with utter scorn – 'I am and will be master, and you shall not live to judge my deeds!' There was silence for a moment. Trembling, the boy waited for the final blow to fall. Then in a shriek of pure madness and lust the Voice cried: 'Now you will hand over the jewel! Now, I tell you!' Terrified though he was, Ivan knew beyond doubt at that moment that whatever happened he would not, could not, give it up: if he must die, let him die with it clutched in his hand. But now the hated voice had become a beguiling whisper in his ear: 'Come, Ivan, it will be so much better if you choose to obey my will. It is mine in any case; but give it willingly and I shall reward you well! When I am master of all, you shall have part of my kingdom'.

Struggling with all his might against the powerful enchantment he felt upon his spirit, he roused himself to shout: 'Never, Voice! Destroy me with your wicked might if you must, but never think that you can make me your servant! I am a servant of the King! You have taken all I held dear, but you can never, never gain my soul!'

'Silence, fool!' screamed the Voice. 'I did not bring you here to the throne-hall of my kingdom to listen to your words of madness! You cannot defeat me, cannot, I tell you! You are in my power, and the jewel is mine!'

His eyes blazed with madness. 'Now for the last time, I order you to hand over the gem!' His shriek filled the cavern. Ivan did not move. 'Now you shall see my power, creature!', screamed the Voice, beside himself with fury. 'The torch above you shall become as a firebrand from hell to destroy both you and the rock you lie upon!' Instantly there came a great flash and a noise like thunder. Ivan, terrified, half-turned on the stone as an agonising pain spread from his arm through his whole body, while the powerful brand rent the huge rock in two, severing his left arm in a rush of blood and shattered bone.

Lost in the horror of the moment, the boy lay still beside the broken stone, sick and fainting from shock, not daring to look up at the demonic being above. 'Now!' howled the Voice once more, 'hand over the gem!' In that very instant Ivan's failing eyes caught sight of something that lay gleaming, embedded in the heart of the blackened rock – it must surely be, it was indeed, the other half of the gem; and it was lying, intact, beside his whole right hand.

At the same moment, in the very instant of the rending fire, the Voice saw the jewel too. Blood streaming from his wounded side, Ivan with a last mighty effort summoned all his failing strength, and as the Voice wailed in pure madness, he rolled over and set the two parts of the broken crystal together. The ancient gem, riven in the dawn of days, was at once healed; even in his agony, a wave of triumph swept over his weary

heart, and he smiled. Even as the jewel was fused together the
Voice had begun to fade from his sight; yet for the last time his
evil cry rang out in the vile caverns of the Underland; for the
last time the flame of his awful power struck the ruined rock
as a vivid fork of scorching lightning, consuming the one who
lay there in a writhing blaze of fire.

Yet it no longer mattered: he knew death well. Already he
was free, running to meet his King, the true ruler of Pyrus,
running to find Kerry and laugh with her in the flower-filled
meadows of a land that would know darkness no more.

* * *

The night was passing; dawn had come. The plains glowed in
amber light, and dew was scattered like living diamonds upon
the emerald earth; as on the first day of Pyrus' making, the
flowers grew fresh and fair. The weal left by the Voice was not
yet gone, but the ravaged land would heal: the hand of the
King laid in love on the wounded earth would suffice. With
the death of the Fawnleader had come a new promise, a new
beginning, and all would yet be well.

In the darkness of the eastern caves could be heard the first
whispered notes of his song; silent at first, invisible, a skein of
laughing chimes that ran amidst the dimness of the firelit caves,
waking, calling, summoning, leading away, high into the
shadows of the rocks. The child who wept was silent now,
comforted, in a sudden lightness of heart as if some half-known
fear was gone; the ones who had fought and cried amid the
hungry darkness held their peace, and left the pathetic knives
and stones which had been their weapons. And the oldest
began to smile, remembering as from some long-forgotten place
the hope that still burned in the inmost citadels of their ravaged
hearts.

And one by one they went to stand together, far down in the
deep caverns of the mountains, and then as one they began to
move upwards towards the brightness of the dawn: they knew
deep in their souls that the glad time had come for the ancient
promise to be fulfilled. The time of their suffering was ending.
And in the solace of the morning light they reached, a great

surging army of the Unborn, the lovely Strells of Pyrus. From the wailing depths, they came to find their paradise.

They found the emerald land they had glimpsed only in dreams, where the light of the new day was dancing in a thousand thousand golden sunbeams. Theirs was then the pure joy of that glad awakening, theirs the sweet air of the meadows, theirs the trilling song of the skylarks, and the health and promise of the silver streams that rushed from the hills. The sun at first dazzled those eyes that had never known the radiance of summer suns: darkened souls began to find healing amid the gentleness of the verdant grasslands. And as they gathered strength, many ran and played and sang.

In every heart the knowledge was born that the Voice and all his evil minions were no more: his power was forever conquered. They had the will to laugh again, to run and not to grow weary. They were free, and none could take their freedom away.

The full moon came and passed, but no longer did the Priests come, nor would their hideous forms be seen again. The land was healed. But the legend of the brave ones who had given their lives so that Pyrus and the Unborn might be saved would never be forgotten, they who had gone forth from the caves in the bitter winter to seek out the Voice, and who having fulfilled their mission had reached at last the peace of a golden land where there was goodness instead of evil and joy instead of tears, and where the darkness need never again be feared.

Epilogue

Come unto me all ye that labour and are
heavy laden and I will give you rest.

The ancient words had been carved deeply in the thick oak
door. They were stained with the dirt of the streets, and the
rain had dripped into the letters over the years, but they had
not worn away.

It was dark, and very late. All the world slept, but the woman
who now stood under the lintel of the church door could not
sleep; exhausted, ill, longing for rest but finding none, she had
waited there until the storm should be over; she huddled in
her scanty refuge, tracing over and over with her finger the
words which seemed to offer a faint ray of hope in her despair.

On an impulse she tried the handle of the door; to her surprise it opened, and she went in. Here at least she might find
sanctuary for a while. In the quiet darkness she saw a feeble
light burning, and moved gratefully towards it. She had ceased
to weep; there were no tears left, she thought; the springs of
her heart seemed to her as dry as the desert itself. She knew
she had not long to live – if only, somehow, peace were to
come to her anguished soul at last! Outside, the storm still went
on; lightning came in vivid flashes that illumined the walls and
windows, so that the figures in the stained glass were outlined
powerfully each time. Then the thunder rumbled again and it
was dark. She waited quietly, hardly knowing what to do next;
she stood for a few moments in the aisle, and then as a great
flash of lightning lit up the window she was facing, she saw
with utmost clarity the figure who hung there. The light had
gone almost at once, but it seemed to her, as she went to kneel

in the darkness, that she still saw His face. It stayed with her for a long time as she went on kneeling, spent, grateful for the hassock beneath her knees, thankful too for the warmth; she shivered convulsively from time to time.

She did not know then whether she was awake or dreaming, but the kingly face seemed to look into hers, the eyes searching her very soul. Shame filled her then, and she would fain have looked away; she could not bear the loving sadness with which He gazed at her. Her whole wasted life seemed to pass before her as she knelt there, ashamed; surely there could be no forgiveness for such as she. She, Celia, who had worshipped her own beauty, who had sold her very soul for all the things she craved – success, riches, acclaim – and who had cruelly abandoned husband and children, destroyed her own unborn child, that she might enjoy her selfish pleasures. She saw His hands then, wounded by the nails; she herself, she knew, had hammered in those nails – how could she ever hope to find forgiveness?

She wept in utter remorse, whispering over and over again in her despair, 'Forgive me, forgive me'. And to her infinite surprise, the face that looked on hers showed nothing but pure love and forgiveness. She felt herself falling, sinking into a sea of darkness, swept away on a tide from which there would be no awakening.

* * *

Then, as in the depths of a dream, she heard a voice: 'My daughter, arise and behold the dawn! Love is stronger than death'. The words seemed to come from very far away, but the voice was filled with love, and it called her as it were from the brink of darkness. Even in her dream she shook her head; not for her, surely such words of forgiveness and acceptance! But she saw that He beckoned to her with arms wide open in love, and so, hesitantly, she went to His side, and knelt while her tears wet His wounded feet. And as the tears flowed, so pain and bitterness seemed to flow out of her heavy heart and leave it light and free.

At last she dared to raise her eyes and look at Him, and she saw that He was smiling, saw too that He was full of glorious light, as that of the brightest star; seeing that there was no other light that might have shone upon Him, she realised that indeed He was the very Light itself.

'My daughter', He said again softly, 'arise and behold the dawn! Love is stronger than death'. This time she arose at His command, and suddenly there was before her a land of beauty beyond imagining, a land of gold that knew no darkness at all, where there could only be light because of Him.

Then in her dreaming state she saw Him raise His arms, and she saw that blood was falling from His wounded hands; and the blood became a stream which grew and grew until it carried her away from Him, away from His brilliant light, to a dark shore from which she still saw His form. Then she saw that He was still smiling to her, across the gulf which now separated their worlds, looking upon her as a loving, forgiving father might, to an erring daughter who had been forgiven. 'Oh my child', He said then, 'would that I could build your bridge, that I could bring you to the golden land, the land promised to the Unborn at the dawn of days; you cannot yet see the glory of the sun that warms their poor broken hearts at last! But your soul too has been weighed down with grief, and your path has for long been the way of death; and you too shall see the new Pyrus I have formed, in all its beauty; you shall see and be comforted. Have I not made all things well?'

Then it seemed that she opened her eyes and caught the glimmer of the rising sun, a sun that arched over His silhouette, high above His uplifted arms, a sun that was the glory of His might, of His own making. Far, far below her in the golden land she saw the mountains, flaming in the radiance of the dawn, their crests crowned with snow; and then nearer, the plains on which a myriad flowers grew. And then she saw people coming, little children running and laughing, running towards the King, the One who by His own terrible suffering had set them free.

And she saw that there was one who led them, a young man whose hands seemed to be covered with blood, yet in whose gaunt face joy shone brightly; and by his side walked a lovely maiden. Together they came to the One who had made the dawn, and as they met Him she saw that they knelt before

Him. And He lifted them up to their feet with great gentleness, speaking to them in words which she could not hear.

Then again He turned to her, His face shining like the sun. 'My daughter', He said, and the words were like music, 'you came to me in the last fleeting moments of your life, kneeling in penitence at the foot of my Cross; how could I cast you out? But now it is given to another to bring that forgiveness to you'. His words had the ring of purest love; she longed with all her heart to hold them, to drink them into her parched soul. Tears streaming from her eyes, she turned away, turned so that she seemed now to see only darkness, a deep darkness which no sun could ever dispel.

But then the young man with the wounds seemed to rise before her, one she had often seen in dreams; and striding towards her he opened his arms wide, and enfolded her, and bore her across the great river that separated them.

'Ivan, my child!' she whispered brokenly.

And he replied, over and over again, 'oh mother, my own mother, at last!'

And then, filled with gladness, she opened her eyes wide, and was forever received into the beauty of the land of the King.